KELLEY POWER
TOMBSTORIES

KELLEY POWER

TOMBSTORIES

ENGEN
BOOKS

Published in Canada by Engen Books, St. John's, NL.

Library and Archives Canada Cataloguing in Publication

Title: Tombstories / Kelley Power.
Names: Power, Kelley, author.
Description: Short stories.
Identifiers: Canadiana 20210234393 | ISBN 9781774780503 (softcover)
Classification: LCC PS8631.O8395 T66 2021 | DDC C813/.6—dc23

Distributed by:
Engen Books
www.engenbooks.com
submissions@engenbooks.com

First mass market paperback printing: September 2021

Cover Design: Graham Blair

For Mom and Dad

1

Kinna's car pulled to a stop outside a set of tall wrought-iron gates. "Cramon Cemetery" arched above the entrance in rusted block letters.

"Engine and seatbelts off," she said. The faint vibration from the engine stopped and there were four simultaneous clicks in the car's cabin.

"It's like someone ordered up the weather for us," Sasha said, leaning toward the windshield as her seatbelt retracted into the car's side pillar. "I can't see anything past those gates."

"We're lucky; the fog is supposed to lift by tomorrow morning," Kinna said.

"I'll run the app off my phone, I guess?" Jad asked.

"Sounds good," Kinna said.

"We're all going to stick together, right?" Scott asked. Kinna glanced at him in the rearview mirror. He'd zipped his jacket up to the top, burying his chin in the collar. With his ballcap pulled low over his eyes, he looked like a turtle hiding in its shell.

"As long as your slow ass keeps moving," Sasha said. She reached into her purse and rummaged inside. Her hand emerged with a black disc the size of a quarter. She tilted her palm from side to side, the shiny black surface of the object reflecting the bright dome light. "Doesn't look like much, does it? Exit car," she added and stepped out as her door opened.

"Exit all," Kinna said and the remaining doors swung outward. "I can't wait to see your faces after each one."

Jad grunted as he heaved himself out. "Sasha, you're in the backseat on the way back. I almost died of claustrophobia back there. Bulls don't fit in shoeboxes."

"So witty," she said. "We'll see."

"You owe me for giving you my lab notes," he said over the roof of the car. Sasha shrugged and held her hands out at her sides as she walked backward toward the gates. "And for rubbing your back last night." She turned and kept going. Jad pulled his face down with his hands like he was trying to tug it off.

Kinna laughed. She glanced in the rear-view mirror again. "Scott, can you grab my bag?" She checked the car a final time to make sure nothing was out of place and anything that could be considered valuable was out of sight. As Scott snagged her shoulder bag from the floor between his feet, she stepped onto the parking lot, gravel crunching under her boot.

"Here you go," Scott said, slinging the strap of the bag over her head and onto her shoulder so it slung across her chest. His fingers lingered, adjusting the strap before he smoothed it with the palm of his hand.

"Thanks," Kinna said and turned toward the gate. She breathed deeply through her nose. "Smell that? Salty, like the ocean. I love it when fog smells like that."

"All I get is dead flowers," Scott said. He sniffed again. "Leaf mold."

The entrance to the cemetery looked exactly as it did in the photos and videos she'd seen online: the tall concrete wall stretched out to the left and right until it blended into the dense grey mist. The gates were high, the arrow-tipped ends of their iron bars out of her reach. Sasha was pulling on one, leaning back to put all her meagre weight into it.

"Move aside, tiny," Jad said, grabbing the bars with both hands and pulling until the veins stood out in his neck. He rattled it, the clank of metal muffled in the heavy fog, then stopped, panting. "They're rusted shut. That was a long drive for nothing."

He scanned the wall, talking about boosting someone over, or pulling the car over so he could stand on the hood, Kinna telling him he'd get on the hood of her car over her dead body. Scott walked up to the gate. He sized it up for a second, lifted a small latch holding the two gates together and used a finger to push the left gate open. It swung back silently. He stood aside and waved his arm, inviting the three of them to go in ahead of him.

"Smartass," Jad said, stomping into the graveyard with Sasha on his heels, her flashlight beam bouncing as she snickered.

"This is why we're friends," Kinna said to Scott as she passed him, tapping the beak of his hat with one hand and flicking her flashlight on with the other. "Someone's got to bring the brains to these operations. Do you know how much trouble I'd have gotten into these past ten years without you to fish me out of it?"

"It's just a gate," Scott mumbled, falling in behind her.

They joined Jad and Sasha, who had stopped at the start of a paved trail that disappeared into the dark. The cemetery was unlike any other they'd been in. Orderly rows of low-slung rectangles in pink and black granite squat on small plots at the far edges of what they could see. Toward the centre, the tombstones ranged from thin, chest-high tablets of lichen-covered stone, to pedestals in marbled rock capped with busts of men and women. Here and there, humble markers sat in the shadows of pillared mausoleums. On the steps of one nearby, Kinna stared at a smooth-skulled skeleton adorned with angel wings, hunched over the lax, kneeling body of a bare-breasted woman whose hips were draped in folded cloth. She was clearly meant to be dead. The skeleton's mouth was pressed to the woman's temple. The sculpture was carved from a light-coloured stone that set it off from whatever dark material the steps of the mausoleum were made from. Kinna sucked in a breath as a second beam of light joined hers, revealing the skeleton's hand disappearing into the woman's side, between her lower ribs.

"Bloody hell," Scott said, moving his flashlight from the skeleton's face to the woman's breasts, then panning it across the front of the mausoleum. "That's my first nightmare accounted for when I go to sleep later."

"You didn't have to come, you know," Kinna said, not noticing the flush of red spread over Scott's cheeks.

"Yeah, well, someone had to bring the brains to this operation," Scott said, repeating her earlier words to him.

She laughed and linked her arm with his. She felt

him tense, but he relaxed seconds later, before she could ask him what was wrong. The heat of him warmed her through her thin denim jacket. It helped take the chill off her exposed skin, where the thick haze left a cool sprinkle of moisture.

A flicker of light caught Kinna's eye and she pulled Scott toward Jad and Sasha. The only sounds in the cemetery were the light grind of their feet against the pavement and the couple's muted voices ahead of them. Jad and Sasha's faces were strobe-lit with the mellow light of a blinking projection. "C'mon, you piece of garbage!" Kinna heard Jad say as he slapped the cell phone in his hand.

"It's not a toaster," Sasha said. "You can't caveman it into submission. What happens when you press this?" Sasha asked as she moved to touch the screen.

"Don't touch anything," Jad said, jerking the phone over his head and out of her reach. "You'll screw it up." He looked up at the screen and at the glitching projection that had followed the direction of his phone. After a breath, he dropped his hand and pushed the icon Sasha had been reaching for and the pale blue projection stabilized against the still grey backdrop of static fog. A man in a cravat, waistcoat and buttoned, wide-lapeled tailcoat stared back at them. His snug pants were tucked into knee-high riding boots. Taller than Jad, but narrower through the shoulders, he was the perfect picture of a trim nineteenth-century gentleman. His hair was slicked back from a widow's peak and sharp angled eyebrows lent his deep-set eyes a surprised look. The skin over his sharp cheekbones was pulled tight, creating dark hollows under them that made him look lean. Hungry.

"Welcome to the Cramon Cemetery Experience." His pencil moustache lifted at one corner with his smile and the lines around his eyes and mouth deepened.

"Damn, did anyone else just get goosebumps?" Jad shivered.

Sasha rubbed her hands up and down the puffy sleeves of her bomber jacket and answered, "That's some voice! Sounds like a cat purring and growling at the same time."

"The website wasn't kidding when they called it realistic," Kinna said. She let go of Scott's arm to swish her hand through the projection. The swirl of fog she left behind made it look more alive.

"He's creepy as shit," Scott said. He took a couple of steps left, then twice as many to the right. "His eyes follow you around."

"His eyes look like they follow me, too," Sasha said, mimicking Scott's movements, urging him to move again. "Still following you? He can't look two ways at once. It's an illusion."

Scott opened his mouth to reply, but the projection cut him off.

"I am your host, Percivet Cinn. Our cemetery has been in use for more than 300 years. The stories of death and loss attached to our residents are as varied as the tombs and memorials that surround you." He clasped his hands in front of his chest, leaned toward them and cocked an eyebrow. "That is what has brought you here tonight, is it not, Ms. Chaytor, Mr. Erim, Mr. Mahoney, and Ms. Balakov — our stories?"

"What the hell?"

"How does he know our names?"

"Awesome."

Kinna held up her hands to quiet her friends. "You all signed up for this through your ChatterBox profiles, remember? They have all your info. They probably know what shoes you're wearing and your pets' names."

Scott pointed to a random spot in the distance. "If I see a projection of Yogi running through this graveyard, I'm out."

"If I see a projection of your dead St. Bernard running through this graveyard, I'm going to shit my pants, buddy," Jad said, patting Scott on the shoulder.

"Shh, something's happening," Sasha said. Cinn opened his arms as if for a hug and a map of blue-lit lines and shapes unfurled, hovering in mid-air. Two wide pathways met at the middle of the map, forming a cross. That was the main nod to order in the vast layout of the cemetery. Almost everywhere else, crooked paths forked off in all directions, the squares and rectangles marking graves were jumbled together like smooth-sided puzzle pieces grouped in irregular blobs and shapes. Six stars spun at different places on the map. Sasha pointed to a large red dot pulsing on the display. "This must be us," she said.

"And the stars are where we'll do the stories," Kinna added.

Cinn nodded, dropped his hands, and began walking. The map floated in front of him for seconds as if supported by an invisible table, then dissolved into the mist. The headstones in his way passed through his body, the projection light illuminating epitaphs on the stones too quickly for Kinna and the rest to read them. He reached a gravel path to their left and stopped moving forward, even though his legs were still in motion. His image flickered. Jad turned to follow him and kept the phone pointed ahead. Cinn started moving forward again and introduced the simulation.

"At each stop you will see torment or death: horrors our residents survived — or did not. Killings they witnessed. Death they caused." Cinn put a finger to his chin. "Perhaps best to say you will experience our interpretation of these events." He chuckled.

Cinn reminded Kinna of every moustache-twirling cartoon villain she'd seen as a kid. The sim was clearly aiming for a caricature of a sinister Victorian gentleman, something right out of Edgar Allan Poe, but the fluidity of his movements, the quality of his voice – everything except the occasional flicker of his projection – made him feel too real to laugh at. She hadn't wanted to say before, but she thought Scott was partly right: it wasn't that Cinn's eyes loosely followed your movements; they looked directly at you, as if he could see *you*, individually. She hadn't imagined that level of interactive tech. She put her hand in her pocket and touched the smooth disc there. What would it be like when things really got started?

Cinn stopped at a thin, waist-high tombstone with a curved top. Jad, Sasha, Kinna and Scott stopped, too, creating a small semi-circle. In their flashlight beams, the marker looked to be made from a solid piece of black stone with veins of bright pink. It was blank. They must be looking at the back, Kinna thought. She began running her thumb over the smooth disc in her pocket. Jad was shifting his weight from foot to foot and Sasha's left hand was fisted at her side. Kinna glanced at Scott out of the corner of her eye. His chin was back inside his coat collar.

"Please put on your Virtoken," Cinn said.

Kinna took the device from her pocket and placed it on the soft, bare skin on the back of her neck, just below her hairline. Her flesh tingled where the disc touched it. The others did the same. Except Scott. He'd put away his flashlight and was holding his disc in his palm. Kinna thought it looked like a burned Communion wafer. A laugh gurgled up her throat and she coughed it down. She hadn't noticed until then how the muscles in her arms and legs were tight, or her heart was beating faster than normal. She grabbed Scott's free hand. He tilted his head up enough for her to see he was biting on his lower lip. She nodded and squeezed his fingers. He reached behind his head, put the disc in place, and his lids lowered.

"There is no need to close your eyes." Scott's opened at Cinn's words and Kinna felt a crushing pressure on her fingers. "Virtoken will take over your retinal stimulation." Sasha hooted and Jad tugged her closer to wrap his arm around her. Kinna was sure Cinn turned his head to look directly at her when he smiled and said, "Some of you may find the immersive experience disturbing. Good luck."

Butterflies fluttered to life in her stomach and the world went black.

INVASIVE SPECIES

Every home has quirks. The buzz of the heating vent in the bathroom, the knock the toaster needs to pop the toast all the way up. Things you get used to hearing or doing day after day. At Annie's house, the third step from the top of the staircase creaked. Pictures on the dining room wall were crooked at the end of day from the neighbours in the connected townhouse shutting their front door. The trap door to the crawl space under her house seized in the summer when it got humid.

Annie knew the quirks in her house inside out. The scratching coming from across the kitchen wasn't one of them.

Thursday morning. Fifteen minutes until she had to jump on the school bus. She was sitting at the kitchen table spreading peanut butter on a slice of whole wheat bread when the wispy scraping caught her ear.

"Did you hear that?"

Her father turned from the newspaper spread on the kitchen counter, a cup of tea halfway to his mouth. "What?"

It came again and she zeroed in on the fridge by the

porch door. She pointed with her knife. "That. Scratching."

"Probably Chester doing something in the living room." Her father slurped the tea and turned back to his paper, reaching for the sugar bowl.

"It's not *in* the other room. And Chester never came home last night." She put down the knife and tilted her head, focusing on the fridge. Her father cocked his head, too, but kept his back to her. "Ah ha! There. You had to hear it that time." Annie scrambled up from her chair, her flip-flops slapping on the tiles as she went toward the fridge. The metal was cool against her ear when she pressed it to the side of the appliance. Its humming made her teeth vibrate.

"Could be a mouse," she heard her father say behind her, clicking his spoon against the sides of the tea mug to blend in the extra sugar he'd added. "Been a while since we had the exterminator in."

Annie was processing the thought of a tiny beady-black-eyed creature under the fridge, inches from her feet, when something grazed her bare ankle. She screamed and took flight, lifting both feet off the ground as she leapt sideways, swiping her hands against her ankles, her feet, her calves. Through the tangle of hair over her eyes, she glimpsed her father, fists on his knees, his rolled newspaper scrunched up in one hand. His face flushed red with the effort to suck in air against the force of the laughter trying to burst out.

"Your face! Jumped so high when I touched you, I thought—" That's all he could manage before conceding to a rolling old-man laugh.

Annie straightened her hair and t-shirt, sliding her right foot back into the flip-flop it had abandoned in front of the fridge. She slanted a look at her father meant to boil his brain. Without a word, she snatched her cell phone off the table and her backpack off one of the chairs and stomped to the back door. The soft sucking slap of flip-flop soles did not make for a dramatic exit.

"I'll see you—" Another deep guffaw cut her father off. He cleared his throat. "After school!"

Annie barely heard him over the extra hard slam she gave the back door on her way out.

"Gross," Karun said around a mouthful of chicken and rice. "Do you need to sleep over tonight? I wouldn't be able to sleep in a house that had mice."

Annie tapped her fork on the cafeteria table. She'd lost her appetite for the fries she'd bought before she sat down with her best friend. "It might not be mice," she said. "Dad just, well, I told you what he did with the newspaper, after he said it could be a mouse. Jerk. He was probably joking."

Karun smiled. "Great prank. Don't roll your eyes! It was." She fake tangled her feet under the table, trying to bring to life the image of Annie's flight from the kitchen. "I wish I could've seen you. Hey!" She sat up straight. "Did I ever tell you about the time a rat got into our basement? Gnawed through the screen in one of the windows. My mother saw holes chewed in the dog food bag and sent my father down with a headlamp to deal with it. You know what it's like down there."

Annie knew. She'd spent hours in that unfinished basement with Karun, digging through boxes and Rubbermaid containers, looking for dirty magazines or booze or anything else parents didn't want kids to find. The couple of naked lightbulbs hanging from the ceiling didn't do anything to brighten up the space. She and Karun always took a flashlight. It spooked her out sometimes, but it wasn't as bad as the crawl space under Annie's house. A two-foot-high, airless void with a dirt floor, reeking of mold. She'd live in Karun's basement before she'd go into that place.

"What do you mean 'deal with it'? Like, your mom sent your dad down to set traps?"

Her mother was a bit worked up about it, Karun explained. While she went off to buy traps, she'd sent Karun's dad down to get a head start on the extermination. He made himself a spear: a broom handle with a nail in the bottom. Cut the head off the nail so it'd be pointy, like those things guys use to pick up litter, she said. "When Mom was a little girl, a rat got into her house and one day she saw it going across the kitchen floor dragging a whole loaf of bread. She's terrified of them.

"Anyways, Dad's in the basement and he's shining the light around, using the stick to knock boxes and poke suitcases and stuff. And all of a sudden," Karun slapped her palms on the table, "it runs across his foot."

Annie jumped and punched Karun on the shoulder for punishment. "He reacted before he even thought about it. Kicked it and it flew across the room and smacked into the concrete wall." She dragged her hands across the table, her skin squealing against the smooth wood. "Fell on the floor, dead."

"So, I tell you I'm freaked out that there could be a mouse in my house and you tell me a story about a rat in yours. Seriously."

Karun sat back in her chair and shrugged. "Just want you to be ready, in case it's something worse", she said. "Whatever it is, it won't come into the house while Chester's there anyway."

"He's not there," Annie said. "He didn't come home last night. I have to check with Mrs. McMann when I get home."

Chester sometimes stayed with the neighbours, especially if they cooked something tastier than what Annie or her dad had on the menu, which seemed like every day this week. Since the weekend, he hadn't eaten anything at home and hardly got off the couch when he was there. It occurred to Annie that maybe he wasn't feeling well. Or maybe the McManns made roast beef this week. That was his favourite. If the smell of beef and gravy found its way to him, Annie would be fighting a losing battle to get him to eat at home until the McManns' leftovers were gone. She wasn't going to wrestle him out of there. They always said he was no trouble. Good for him. Ate like a king.

After the school bus dropped her off, Annie stopped at the McManns' townhouse and knocked on the gleaming sunflower-yellow front door. Their doorbell had been broken for months. Dad said Mr. McMann was getting old and didn't take care of things the way he used to. When no one answered, she knocked again and looked through the stained-glass sidelight. It was impossible to make out details, but she knew the house was a mirror image of hers: behind the door was a small porch and, beyond that, a hallway with a staircase that went to the second floor. A cluster of doors led off the hallway: one to the living room, one to the dining room, and one to the kitchen.

She knocked a third time when she thought she saw a shadow move at the end of the hall, near the squiggly orange outline of what would be the kitchen door. Annie turned and looked at the McManns' car in the driveway, at the bird poop covering the hood and windshield, as if nobody had cared to clean it off in days, and wondered if maybe they'd gone away. They usually told her dad so he could keep an eye on their house. She made a mental note to ask him when he got home. Because if they were gone away, that left another question: where the hell was Chester?

She jumped off the front step and went next door, into her house.

It was her turn to make dinner. Annie checked the time on her phone and saw she had a window between when her dad got home from the lumber yard and when she had to get started on the spaghetti. She went into the kitchen to grab a Dr Pepper and saw a couple of glue traps her father had put down under the cupboards closest to the fridge. Another was in the rear porch, partially hidden by the long grassy bristles of a broom. He wasn't kidding, then; it was a mouse. Dammit. She wished she was wearing something sturdier than flip-flops. Sneakers. Ski boots.

She slid a loaf of bread off the counter – no rodent was

getting into *her* sourdough – and tip-toed to the fridge, grabbing the handle. Holding her breath, she popped the seal on the refrigerator door. She stopped to listen for any scratching or squeaking. There was nothing like the sound she heard this morning, only the gentle humming of the fridge. Letting her breath out, she swung the door open all the way and a waft of garlic and fish crawled up her nose. At eye-level was a plate of salmon her father had cooked last night. The bag of bread fit on the shelf next to it. She searched the shelves for the burgundy-brown can she wanted, pushing aside jam jars and the leftover fish.

"Gotcha," Annie said, closing her hand around the cold can. At the same second she felt a tickle on the tip of her big toe.

The plate of salmon was the first thing to take flight. It was launched out of the fridge by the force of her fist whipping backward as her body violently put distance between itself and the sensation of being touched. The smash of the plate against the tiles was barely audible over her screams; not a single, long piercing announcement of fright, but a rhythm keeping time with her rushing breath. The tin of Dr Pepper went airborne next, shooting out of her hand when her back came up hard against the edge of the kitchen table. It hit the back of the wooden chair with enough force to puncture the thin tin. A thread of brown liquid jetted out of the hole and blasted everything, including Annie, on the can's way to the floor. It spun for a second and came to a stop in a frothy brown puddle. The pop on her face jarred her from her screaming fit. She bent for the can, whipped it up and dropped it in the sink, tossing the dishcloth on top in case it got any ideas about starting up like a fire hose again.

A safe few feet from the fridge, Annie scanned the carnage. Fragments of the plate sat at the centre of a bullseye of pink flakes of salmon, clumps of mashed potatoes and green beans. Where the food spattered onto the unopened freezer door near the floor, it mixed with rivulets of Dr Pepper. The sticky soft drink had painted the kitchen table, chairs, wall and nearby cupboards with a fine spray. Annie spotted a few droplets on the white ceiling. Lording over it all was the open fridge door. It looked like the refrigerator had vomited up the lot of it.

Her focus, though, was the narrow gap at the base of the fridge. *Mouse. Rat. Mouse. Rat.* They were the only words her brain would allow. She stared so long, her eyes dried, along with the sticky brown soft drink on her cheek and forehead.

When she saw *it*, she was sure it was a trick of her arid eyes.

If it were smaller, she could have mistaken it for the rusty-orange centipedes that skitter away from overturned rocks and tipped flower pots. But with its body as big around as her thumb, and wider still from the uncountable yellow spikes – legs? – twitching along its body, it was like no insect she'd seen before. Was it even a bug? At least six inches of it had slipped out from under the fridge. No, ten. More was slithering out by the second. Annie's jaw went slack as she watched it stretch and probe through the mash of food on the floor. The Dr Pepper tin chose that moment to gurgle in the sink. Annie screamed and spun around and kept spinning until she was facing the fridge again because damned if she was going to keep her back turned on whatever was creeping out across the floor. Except it wasn't creeping anymore. It was frozen. Reared in the air like a cobra in striking position, pointing in her direction.

It didn't have eyes, at least none that Annie could see, but the part of her brain responsible for making the hair stand up on the back of her neck and her stomach tighten in a knot knew that it was watching her. The adrenaline rush left her body vibrating with tingles. She'd always thought of herself as a "fight" kind of person when it came to danger, but dread coursed through her - mortal dread, the kind a calf must feel when she's being run down by a wolf pack – and Annie couldn't get her muscles to react.

The creature's legs twitched and more of its ruddy, insectile body slid soundlessly from under the fridge. Its narrow tip rose higher until it was at Annie's eye-level. It swung in tiny arcs, its legs grasping at the air. Annie stared. Her heart rate slowed and some of the tension left her arms and legs. There's nothing to be afraid of, she told herself, watching the creature swing side to side. Was it closer? Yes. Close enough to brush against her cheek, the corner of her open mouth, her lips. Didn't matter. It didn't mean her any harm. It tickled. A spurt of energy tried to rinse away her inertia, a final cry to run, run, run far away, but it petered out with the gentle rhythm of the creature's movement. A scent prickled her nose. Sharp. Burning. It reminded her of something, but she couldn't put her finger on it. It got stronger, making her eyes water.

A faint sound from the hallway behind her pricked her awareness. *Click.* The creature stilled. What would it feel like to touch it? Her arm lifted without her meaning to do it. A louder click behind her and the jangle of keys. Her arm was still moving, but the thing was, too. Backwards. She wanted to tell it to stop, but her mouth stayed slack and still.

"Hi there, ho there." Her father's baritone was like an electric shock, striking life back into her limbs, her face. She blinked a half-dozen times, fast flickers, watering up her eyeballs for the first time since that thing crept out. Her father's heavy-booted footsteps thumped up the hall. "Annie? Stinks like fish in here." His voice was nearby, almost at the kitchen door. "How come you're standing there like that?" She realized he could see her standing in the kitchen near the sink, statue-like, with the fridge hidden from sight around the corner.

The thing – call it a monster, Annie; you know it is – dropped to the tiles and shaped itself into a loop around the mass of ruined food in front of the fridge. With a quick jerk, it disappeared under the appliance, taking half the mess with it, piling the other half up against the bottom of the freezer door.

"What the f—" was as much as her father got out before Annie's moaning huff of air cut him off and she collapsed to her knees on the floor. Every organ in her body felt like it was competing to eject itself from her mouth first. Her head spun and she started to pant. It was her first panic attack.

It was no use talking to her father. She realized this when she told him what happened and the explanation he came up with was how he'd poked under the fridge with the straw broom earlier to scare out a mouse, if there was one, and obviously a few strands had come off and gotten left under the fridge until she stirred them up and one poked out enough to graze her foot and got caught in her flip-flop and looked like it was moving by itself and ha, ha, wasn't it all really funny?

"And what about it touching my face?" Annie had asked him.

"Oh honey, you were so worked up by then, you could've seen the devil himself standing there and thought it was real. Do you know what panic does to a brain?" Dr. Dad, M.D. and sawmill foreman, had proceeded to tell her. She wished she'd called him a stupid dick the minute he'd started doubting her, instead of waiting until the end of his bullshit diagnosis, so he could've sent her to her room before she'd gagged on his condescension.

And before she'd had to clean up the kitchen.

But he didn't take her phone away when he sent her upstairs and for that she was grateful. She had to tell Karun what happened. She couldn't risk her father hearing her on the phone, so stuck to texting. But there was *so much* to tell. Her thumbs had never moved so fast across the keypad. Once she got through the bulk of the story, it got easier.

Karun: *ur sure you didn't hit your head?*

Annie: 👆

Karun: *LOL had to ask, its nuts*

Annie: *u dont think I know that?*

Karun: *what r u gonna do?*

Annie put the phone down next to her and lay back on

her bed. Good question. She couldn't pretend like it never happened. The memory of the creature in the kitchen sat heavy on her mind. It wasn't the thing itself that bothered her. Okay, that was a lie. An enormous centipede thing with a mind of its own crawling out from under the fridge was definitely freaky. Worse, though, was the way it came to her. Wanted to hurt her. She couldn't explain how she knew, she just did, in her molecules. And she hadn't done anything to stop it. No running, no struggling. Gave in and waited for it to happen. Reliving it stirred up a deep vulnerability. She swallowed and was surprised to feel heat build across her cheeks. Her eyes welled up. Crying? Hell no.

She wiped her eyes with the back of her hand and picked up her phone. Karun's last text sat in a bubble, waiting. Annie's fingers moved across the screen, the haptic response of the phone making it jump in her hands as she typed.

Karun: *what r u gonna do?*
Annie: *kill it*

Annie's first approach with her father – telling the truth – had been doomed to fail. Dan Fitzgerald was a practical man. He didn't believe in God or ghosts or electric cars. She needed his help for what she had in mind and that meant changing her tune.

"Daddy?" She said it softly as she came down the stairs. He sat in his recliner in the living room, bearded face lit with a flashing jumble of light from the television screen.

"Don't want to hear it, Annie. You can't disrespect me like that without consequences." He turned to face her and pointed a finger at her. "That's the trouble with your crowd: all your Twitting and Snip Chatting and What's Happeninging – you're not learning how to have proper conversations with people and be accountable for what you say and do."

Annie bristled, but didn't correct any of his mistaken names of the chat apps she and her friends used. Fighting with him wasn't going to get her what she wanted. She took a deep breath. "I wanted to say I'm sorry." She swallowed around the lie.

He dropped his hand.

"I shouldn't have said what I did. I..." she cleared her throat. "I was afraid. Of the mouse." It took everything in her not to roll her eyes at herself. Naturally, she didn't want one running up her leg, but it was a blow to her pride admitting she melted down over a mini-rodent when something far more dangerous was to blame. Her father swiped the recliner's handle and the leg rest dropped with a tumble of mechanisms. He turned to face her. Annie sensed him softening. She stood in the living room doorway. "I got confused when the broom straw stuck out and all the food and stuff was flying everywhere and I even thought I saw it, the mouse, run at me." As an afterthought, she added a shiver. That put her father over the edge. He sprang out of the chair and folded her into a bear hug, apologizing for being so hard on her. Being disrespectful wasn't okay, he said, but he understood and she was too delicate to face down a mouse. She gritted her teeth and let him have his moment. When he kissed her on the forehead and finally relaxed his arms enough to make some space between them, she sighed heavily and looked down at a button on his plaid shirt.

"Do you think we could pull the fridge out to take a look at what's in there?" This is what she needed from him: his muscle. She wanted a good look under that fridge. "I think it would help me sleep."

"You sure you want to do that, honey? I don't want you having another fit." Her anger flared but was muffled when she looked up and saw his furrowed eyebrows and the clear concern in his face. She imagined what he had seen when he'd come home: her slack-jawed and seized, suddenly falling to the floor in a panicky heap in the middle of the messy calamity she'd created. He wasn't good with emotion at the best of times; she'd really tested his limits this evening. She took his hand and smiled up at him with genuine affection.

"I'm sure." This wasn't only for her, after all. If something dangerous was in the house, it could hurt him, too, and all they had was each other. She needed to get to the bottom of it.

"All right. Let's take a look." He dropped her hand and led the way to the kitchen. Over his shoulder he asked, "Have you seen Chester? We could use a hand with this. It's right up his alley."

She hadn't thought about him since she'd left the McManns' doorstep. "No. I tried next door after school but nobody answered. Did they go out of town?"

"Not that they told me. I knocked on their door to drop off a piece of mail that ended up in our box, but same thing. I don't think I've seen them in a couple of days."

As Annie passed the dining room, she looked at the pictures on the wall, the ones she always had to adjust after a day of the McManns going in and out their front door. They were perfectly straight. Now that she thought about it, she hadn't touched them in a few days. If McManns weren't home, where was Chester? He was capable and independent but she didn't like the idea of him being gone for a couple of days.

She thought up a list of people to call and places to look for him as she walked into the kitchen and sat on the table across from the fridge, her feet planted on the cool wooden chair seat. Her dad went to the fridge, touching it in various places, looking for the best handholds. The appliance was nestled between two countertops, so had to be pulled straight out. As she watched his big, burly frame brace and start to roll the fridge forward, she thought about how he'd always taken care of her, raised her himself after her mom died, never asked her for more than good grades and a good attitude. A wave of nausea rolled through her and the terror of losing him blew a chill through her. This was wrong. Risky. What if the creature was there waiting? What if it got inside his head like it had hers? What if it hurt him? Took him?

"Daddy, wait," she said, words tight with tension, but he already had the fridge a foot away from the wall. "Wait!" she yelled. It clunked across the tiles until it was all the way out.

"It's fine, honey," he said. "It's okay. I knew this was a mistake. Too much for you. I'm sorry." He poked his head around the side of the fridge. "I'll put this back in a… Damn it!"

Annie jumped off the table. She didn't ask her legs to do it, they just took her to her father, driven by an urge to save, to fight this time. His broad shoulders blocked the right side of the fridge. She sprang to the left and leaned over the counter, fists up, to take on what was waiting. The tiles under the fridge were smeared with bits of pink, white and green - remnants of the salmon dinner that had been scooped under the fridge by the centipede thing. In the corner where the wall met the cupboard there was a tennis ball-sized hole in the floor.

"We've got a rat, honey. A mouse couldn't chew through the tiles like that. We're gonna need some bigger traps."

If what she saw earlier was a rat, it had some serious genetic problems. Bigger traps weren't going to help.

He hauled his big frame onto the counter and dropped onto the small square space behind the fridge. "Pass me your phone," he said. "I need some light." Annie held it out to him, her hand shaking. He squatted and shined the light into the hole. "Yep, definitely tracks and disturbance in the crawl-space dirt. Looks like something big was dragged around down there. Smell that?" Her father leaned closer to the floor.

"Dad, stop. Don't."

"Ack!" He reared back and Annie jerked, reaching for him. "Might be one dead down there. The smell is like that time your grandma put out poison for the mice and one rotted in her walls. Remember?" He mock-gagged. "But this is worse." He bent for another sniff and recoiled from the hole, and Annie's heart leapt into her throat. He started coughing and pressed the back of his hand to his face. The cell light shone up into Annie's eyes, blinding her.

"What? What is it?" She backed away and blinked the flashes of light out of her eyes.

He coughed. "Ammonia. Probably cat piss. They must be getting in around the cladding, going after the rats."

Ammonia. That was the smell Annie couldn't identify earlier in the kitchen. She smelled it outside the house all the time. The neighbourhood was riddled with cats and they loved to come to her house. She was convinced Chester brought them home with him.

"Weird for rats to come around with that much cat activity. Must be the king rat. Nicodemus." He laughed and passed back her phone, wiggled his fingers at her in a fake-spooky way. Annie wanted to find his throwback to *The Secret of NIMH* funny, but she was focused on piecing together what they'd learned. There was something under the house, it came up through a hole in the floor into the kitchen, it was interested in food, it looked like a centipede out of a nightmare, and everything smelled like cat pee. The sensible part of her brain told her there was one piece of information that didn't belong; the piece only she had experienced: the creature from hell. If she dropped that one piece out of the equation, everything else added up perfectly and pointed to what her father said: there was a rat (please, only one) under the house, it came up into the kitchen, and cats were getting into the crawl space, chasing it.

Her father was talking about getting an exterminator in tomorrow, checking out the cladding around the base of the house to see where rodents could be getting in, and talking to the McManns when he saw them. He went down through the problem-solving list one item at a time as Annie catalogued her own list of facts. She opened the texting app on her phone and sent Karun a message.

Annie: *its a rat*
Three shimmering dots appeared immediately, then,
Karun: *faaaaaaaaaaaahhhhhhhhhhhhhhk*
Annie: *yep im an idiot*

She and Karun shot messages back and forth. Annie was aware of her father hoisting himself back over the counter and settling in front of the fridge to push it back into place.

"Hey, Annie." She stopped and looked up. "Do you hear that?"

She listened. "No, I don't hear anything." Her thumbs flashed over the keypad for a second, then she looked up and said, "It'd be really mean if you're trying to scare me again."

"I'm not. Wait." They both stood silently. A faint moan floated from behind the fridge. "There. That." They waited, leaning over the counters. The sound came again. Stronger. It wasn't a moan. It was a meow. Guttural. The sound a cat makes when it's facing down a trespassing feline, or watching a crow get frisky outside the window. But it had a catch at the beginning. A familiar catch that came from a cat with the damaged voice box he'd had since he was a kitten.

"Chester?" Annie said. The meow came again. "Chester!" She looked at her father. "He sounds wrong. Is he okay? Will a rat attack a cat?"

"If it's cornered. I guess we know where he's been the last couple of days. Probably got himself trapped in there. Let's see if we can get him to come in through the crawl space door."

Annie was afraid of opening the trap door. She'd seen videos of rats jumping as high as three feet in the air. Imagining one flying through the crawl space door into the house had her palms sweating. But she wanted Chester back, safe. Her father was already moving to the back porch where the door was. He pushed aside the boots and shoes on top of it and jerked the handle. It creaked but didn't open. Humidity had it swelled shut. He gave it another tug, throwing his weight behind it, and it came loose. He was off balance, so he went backwards with the door, smacked his head on the wall with a firm *crack* and collapsed onto the floor with the door on top of him. The clothes rail in the porch was shaken loose and all the coats slid down over him, too. Under the tangle of cloth, Annie could see tiny movements, but he wasn't trying to throw off the clothes or stand. She replayed the awful sound of his head hitting the wall and thought he must be dazed. Unconscious? She rushed the few feet forward to help him, but Chester sprang up from the trap door, between them, and she slid to a stop.

"Hey Chessie," she bent and rubbed a hand down his back, getting ready to pick him up, move him away from the opening in the floor. His thick fur was matted with mud in places, caked in dark copper clumps in others. She sifted through it and felt lumps the size of grapes along his flesh. One quivered under her fingers. Her body erupted in gooseflesh. She stumbled backward, feet tangling. Her backside hit the floor hard enough to snap her teeth together.

Chester meowed, rawer and more guttural than before. His green eyes were wide, their whites shot with pink streaks. A spatter of bright red hung in his chin fur. His body convulsed and rippled. The centipede creature poked out of his tangled coat and slithered Annie's way. Her bare feet squealed across the tiles as she used her heels to push herself away from it. A second creature erupted from Chester's fur. A third. Her stomach clenched. The smell of ammonia flooded her nose as she sucked in a lung-full of air; it sat on the back of her tongue like a skin. Her shriek echoed through the kitchen.

A rustle behind the cat caught her eye. Her father's hands were slowly pushing and pulling at the coats covering him. She called to him. His muffled reply was lost under the cloth. The thing that used to be Chester shook and a dozen more wiggling spiked creatures reached out of his body and went straight for Annie. Her ankles and thighs were snagged in coils of sharp, prickling spikes. One wound itself around her throat and drove deep into her skin. She felt herself being pulled across the floor, but there was no pain. No feeling at all. Her mind free-floated. Her view of her father, struggling to stand, crawling across the floor toward the cat, started to blacken at the edges, sprinkled with small starbursts. He spoke, but it came to her in slow motion. Couldn't understand.

The Chester-creature was twisting her legs, building pressure around her neck. Something in her body snapped. She didn't know if she felt it or heard it.

Her vision shrank to a tiny circle. Through it she saw the cat-thing's mouth open unnaturally wide, its jaw un-hinged, and four nested circles of jagged teeth wriggled inside. Her father's muffled voice reached her. He was saying her name. But it was hard to hear anything over the blood rushing in her ears and the squelch of some-thing juicy. Her last thought was to wonder what part of her body it was.

2

Jad handed his phone to Sasha and puked into the grass at his feet. "Oh God, oh God, I barfed on someone's grave. I'm sorry! So sorry!" He heaved again.

"That never happened." Kinna rubbed her eyes as she spoke, trying to erase the afterimage of the young girl being eaten alive by what used to be her cat.

Scott rubbed his throat. "Are we supposed to feel anything physical? For a minute at the end, I was having trouble breathing."

"I didn't feel anything," Sasha said. "You were pretty keyed up when we started, Scott. You probably held your breath. It was definitely intense enough. Even better than I imagined!"

Cinn nodded, as if accepting the compliment.

"Yeah, but it wasn't how that girl really died," Kinna said. "That creature was made up. What was it supposed to be anyway? Random."

Jad spit and wiped his mouth with the back of his hand. "Sorry! Now I'm spitting on graves. Is this place Catholic? Should I do one of those chest cross things?" His hands moved in a Z from his shoulders to his hips.

"Don't you guys remember hearing about this a few years ago? Some guy killed his kid and said the cat did it. Told the cops the thing was possessed and had all these tentacles flying out of it."

"Right!" Sasha said. "They also got him for killing his neighbours. They were buried under the house. He blamed that on the cat, too."

"So, the guy was bonkers," Kinna said. "What we saw was a spin on the real story."

"The world is full of strange and unexplained things," Cinn said.

"I remember them saying the cat never did turn up," Sasha said. "They figure the guy killed it."

"Probably ate it," Jad said and dry-heaved.

"Seriously, Jad," Scott said.

"Each simulation will leave you deciding for yourself which elements were real and which were not." Cinn walked around to the front of the headstone. "I did say there was an interpretive element to the stories, but that does not mean they are untrue."

Kinna followed him and looked down at the headstone. Jad, Sasha and Scott, clearing his throat sporadically, came around to look. The smooth black front of the stone was engraved with a spray of stars across the top with a scripted epitaph below:

Of all the stars in the sky
Yours burned the brightest

Annie M. Fitzgerald
June 12, 2008 – September 18, 2023

Sasha made an angry noise in her throat and pointed. "Oh, hell no. What twisted mind did that?" At the base of the grave marker was a cast concrete cat lying down with its head up, as if keeping guard over the girl in the ground under him. Cinn wiggled a finger and a blue-hued centipede skittered across the face of the tombstone.

"So, so wrong," Scott added.

Cinn chuckled. He waved his hand and the map unrolled in front of him. The star at their current stop was no longer spinning. The active star closest to their blinking red dot was among a set of lines laid out in one of the cemetery's few symmetrical grids. "Your next story awaits." He started walking. Kinna and the other three fell in behind him. "Please leave your Virtokens in place. They will not activate until we are ready to begin a new tale."

"Great," Scott said. "It's probably collecting all my vital signs. If I start getting texts advertising vitamin supplements or gym memberships, I'm going to be pissed, Kinna."

She wasn't listening. Kinna was reliving parts of Annie's story. The virtual experience was more visceral than she'd expected. More than once she'd had the sensation of standing in the same room with the characters. People. They were based on real people, real stories, she reminded herself.

"Look at how he walks," Sasha snagged her attention with an elbow to the ribs. "Like he's floating, or on a conveyor belt. It's creepy."

"That's what's creeping you out?" Kinna asked. "Not reliving a real life murder? Or mutilation. Whatever it was."

"Nah. Don't take it so seriously. It's made-up stories with some real names and places used to make it juicier. No different than watching a horror movie based on real events."

"Except it's like watching it happen in real time," Scott said. Kinna shot him a grateful glance. At least it wasn't only her.

Cinn led them through the tombstones as they swapped opinions on their first experience in the simulation. He cut down a narrow, mown pathway. Their footsteps kicked up the scent of grass and moist soil. The stones on either side of the path shone in the flashlight beam; high-gloss, polished granites on manicured plots. Some had bouquets of fresh flowers – carnations, roses; a single white calla lily in front of one marker carved in the shape of a hummingbird.

"These are the more recent graves, I bet, like Annie's," Scott said. "None of the older stones we saw were polished or in neat rows like these."

Kinna nodded and added, "None of them had fresh flowers, either; only those old plastic ones. Blech."

"I want someone to plant a tree on my grave," Sasha said. "A big oak. Something that will live for a long time."

"Its roots would grow down into you," Kinna said.

"That's kind of the point, isn't it?" Sasha said, hesitating at a gravestone with a life-sized granite soccer ball sitting on it. "Dust to dust. One with nature and all that crap." She moved on.

Kinna pictured it: fragile stringy roots attaching to the

flesh, sinking into it, thickening, lengthening. "Gak!" She shivered all over.

Sasha laughed. "It's only gross if you imagine it happening to someone who's alive," she said, reading Kinna's mind.

She stopped and the other three looked up. Cinn was standing over a black, doormat-sized marker set flat into the grass. The death date on the stone read September 30, 2021, but its shiny surface was scuffed and chipped more than would be expected for a stone laid only a few years ago. The name of the deceased was sealed under a layer of tar-like black paint, over which someone had painted in careful white block letters: LOST SOUL.

"Damn, that's cold," Jad said.

"I can't figure out if that's meant as an insult, or a tribute," Scott said.

"Perhaps it is both," Cinn said. "Relationships between the living are complex; why would we expect them to be any less so post-mortem?"

"I don't know, I'd have to be pretty pissed to come all the way up here to do that to someone's gravestone," Sasha said.

"Or be in some weirdly deep state of grieving," Kinna replied.

"Let us see what light the actors in this drama can shed on it themselves," Cinn proposed and snapped his fingers.

END OF THE LINE

Nix picked at the dried blood caked on his cuticles.

"Look at this," he said to the stocky guy sitting on the subway seat next to him. His best friend, Aiden, looked up from his phone and peered at the fingers offered for his inspection.

"Why didn't you get rid of that in the gas station?" Aiden asked.

"Uh, because some asshole was beating on the door, telling me the cops pulled into the parking lot?"

Aiden laughed. "Yeah. That was a good one. You burst out of there with your dick practically hanging out of your pants."

"Asshole," Nix repeated. Aiden's laughter deepened. Nix rubbed his fingernails again. No use. He'd end up mangling the cuticles if he kept trying to get the blood off. He'd use the nail brush when he got home.

Aiden held his phone out to Nix and touched the screen. A video played. Blurry first. The image was moving jerkily back and forth, like the person holding the phone was moving. A pair of heavy black combat boots came into frame – the feet of the camera holder - then the image panned up to show two guys with their arms locked around each other, twisting, fists heat-seeking a head or an exposed slab of ribs. One had on a black baseball hat and half his face covered with a bandana of a skull's grinning mouth. The other was a dark-skinned man in a sport jacket, his sunglasses askew on his face. Their shuffling feet kicked and creased a hand-written cardboard sign on the ground: *WHY IS ENDING RACISM A DEBATE?*

Other people ran past chanting and yelling, flowing around the fighters as they would a hornets' nest. Other signs were raised in the air, other faces were covered by scarfs and masks, their words and shapes and colours obscured by thick streamers of smoke drifting across the scene. Skull-face thrust forward and snapped his forehead against the other guy's nose. A loud hoot and a voice off-camera shouted, "Yeah! Get him! Get that n—" with the rest obscured by screaming and scuffling. The injured man cupped his nose and blood seeped down the crease between his hands. Skull-face wrapped an arm around his neck and used the other one to pummel him in the stomach, ribs and chest. The man fell to the pavement face-first when his attacker stopped holding him up. Skull-face put a boot under him and turned him on his back. The man's sunglasses were hanging from one ear. He shook his head side to side. His lips were moving, but if he was speaking, it couldn't be heard over the racket of the crowd swarming past him. The guy in the bandana hunched and levelled cracking blows across both sides of the man's face. When he stopped, the man's lips were slack under the bloody pulp of his face. The attacker swung around yelling, "White Lights! BOOYAH!" into the camera. His grey eyes were wide, scarlet-stained fists held up like a prize fighter.

"A thousand views and it's only been up for a half-hour," Nix said.

Aiden slid his phone into his pocket and leaned back against the windows. "I sent it to Dwight. You're on the stream." He stared at the empty advertising panel on the opposite side of the subway car. After a minute, he said, "Do you think that guy's dead?"

Nix shrugged. "One less whining queer lib-tit. Did Dwight say anything?"

"Not yet. I'm sure he will." Aiden snorted. "Can't imagine that won't satisfy him."

A rough join in the subway tracks bounced Nix's shoulders and knees against Aiden's. The two of them had been friends since they met on the M train when they were thirteen. Both on their way to Cornelius Owens Jr. Academy, Aiden had seen Nixon trying to slide a twenty-dollar bill out of a man's pants pocket. When the dude had looked down and caught him, Aiden had slammed into the guy from behind. The two boys were able to scrape through the closing subway doors before anyone could snag them by their school blazers or backpacks. On the platform, Nix had opened his fist and showed Aiden the twenty. They spent it on burritos and a few smokes they bought off a guy standing outside the liquor store.

The next day they met again on the M and got talking about Nix's retro Air Jordans and Aiden's Apple Watch. Chatted about how their parents had condos in Aspen but Nix and Aiden had never seen each other there on the slopes. They'd skipped the stop for their school and gone down to 10th Street, where Nix's older brother had told him there was a guy in a dollar store who'd sell them weed. They'd rolled it and smoked it behind an Indian restaurant, where they'd smashed empty beer bottles against the building's brick walls until a guy in a stained apron opened the heavy metal backdoor and waved them away with a ladle. Aiden had thrown his last bottle in the guy's direction and it burst into a million brown pieces when it struck the top of the doorframe. Him and Nix were already on the next street over by the time the guy gathered himself and made a run up the alley after them.

The cement for their friendship had been poured and set.

"Speaking of tits," Aiden sat up and grabbed the handles of the duffle bag sitting between his feet. "I'm getting off at Hampton." Nix's eyebrows shot up. "No, I'm not back with Christa. But, I'm *vibrating*, man. I need to put this energy somewhere." He pulled his phone out and flicked through it with his thumb, turning the screen to Nix when he found what he wanted: a picture of a girl smiling into the camera with her shirt pulled up to show her bare body.

"Send me a good vid this time," Nix said. "That last one was garbage. It was too dark to make out her face." He made a sliding motion with his fist, in and out of his mouth.

Aiden laughed and shoved Nix's shoulder. "I've missed this - you and me hanging out." The train started to slow and a voice came over the speaker announcing that the next stop was Hampton Street. Aiden stood and picked up his bag.

"Come to the White Lights meeting Tuesday," Nix said. "I think you made an impression at the last one."

Aiden looked down at him and sighed. "Yeah, I think you're right." The train came to a jerky stop. The doors opened. Aiden swung the bag over his shoulder and walked backward to the exit. "We'll see what happens with the video and...everything." He stopped before he stepped onto the platform. "Maybe if things turn out okay, we can do some tagging soon." He shook the bag and the spray paint cans inside clanked hollowly.

Nix shrugged. "Yeah, maybe." He wouldn't have time to scrawl on synagogues if his video got traction with the right people today. He pointed at Aiden. "And don't dodge; I said I want a video from tonight." Aiden cocked a half-smile and stepped off the train. The sliders closed and the *click-click, click-click* of the M train picked up its tempo. The familiar sound soothed Nix's brain. He pulled up his bandana and adjusted it using his reflection in the window across from him, straightening it out until the partial skull printed on it was aligned with the lower part of his face. He closed his eyes and tipped his head back.

Aiden couldn't see the big picture. What was the end-game in spray-painting swastikas and *sig* runes every-where? That kid stuff him and Aiden got up to was fun, but it didn't have *purpose*. You could throw all the fire-works you liked into some darkies' cell phone store and watch them scurry out like cockroaches, but what was the point when the store stayed open and they kept on breed-ing? Shit was serious now. The leeches were coming into the country in droves, pushing people out of jobs, neigh-bourhoods. The modern day rapers and pillagers. Election laws were all wrong; the immigrants here long enough to vote could band together and get their own kind into government.

The White *Lights* knew the stakes. Dwight King saw it coming twenty years ago and started the organization.

Dwight. He wanted to burn it all down. "Government is broken," he'd shouted at the White Lights rally Nix went to a month ago, the auditorium filled with thousands of nodding heads. "Elections are rigged; who do you think counts the votes?" *Illegals*, the crowd shouted. "Right. The same ones who are pushing you out of your jobs. And what are the liberal elites doing about it?" The mix of answers made it hard to pick one out, but *fuck them* was audible. "Exactly. Nothing. They're in their secret societies, waiting for the kickbacks, infiltrating schools to brainwash your children into carrying rainbow flags. And they think *you're* paranoid." Nix remembered booing with the rest of them. "Well, we're taking this country back. I'm mad as hell!" *And I'm not going to take it anymore*, Nix screamed with thousands of others.

He wasn't expecting his parents to go into a lather when they found out he'd been at the rally. He'd always been open about his take on what was wrong with the world. He'd been brought home by the cops for vandalizing a mosque ("vandalizing" was their word; Nix called what he'd written on the wall a public service announcement). He'd told them he wouldn't be coming to any dinner they had for his cousin Megan and her new husband from Senegal. In those cases, they'd given him a weekend grounding or kept the car from him for a week. No biggie. But the rally?

"I thought you'd outgrow this idiocy, but it's obviously rotting your brain," his dad had said. "The White Nights are this close to being domestic terrorists." He'd held up his thumb and forefinger a hair's breadth apart. "Is that who you are? Is that how we raised you?"

"White Lights. And you mean the idiocy where we're losing control of our country to lib-tits and their dark army?"

His father had grabbed his own hair in both hands and pulled. "Shirly, can you...? I just can't." He sagged into his La-Z-Boy. Mom tried a different angle.

"That man is an anarchist," she'd said about Dwight. "Do you have any idea what real anarchy would look like? You're up there in that comfortable bedroom, safe in this house, with all your expensive gadgets. All that, gone. You'll be in the street with someone gunning you down because they don't like the way you look or you have something they want."

"Only people like you see themselves on the receiving end of the gun," Nix said.

It'd gotten real ugly after that.

It ended with him stuffing his things into a couple of rolling suitcases and waving goodbye to his parents with the shouted hope they'd stop being pawns of the oligarchy. He arrived on Aiden's doorstep tired, but with a restlessness to move, take action, as if he'd shed a weight that had been pressing him to his knees. He called Dwight that night to tell him what had happened. Within a couple of days Dwight had found him a room in an apartment with three other guys. He took a job with the Lights doing errands and some landscaping at Dwight's place. He still saw Aiden when they overlapped on the M train, but today at the protest was the first time they'd hung out together in a couple of weeks.

Nix pulled out his phone and checked Snapchat. No reply yet to the video. He refreshed a couple of times before putting the phone away and closing his eyes again. His knuckles cracked as he flexed his fingers. The adrenaline from the protest and the justice he dished out to finish his initiation into the White Lights was well gone. He caught his chin dipping to his chest. He'd have to be careful not to miss his stop.

What would Dwight say when he saw the video? What would Dwight's daughter, Emmy, say? Nix smiled under his bandana. Emmy. She was the first White Light he'd met. Was it a year ago already? She'd come up to him at a protest against the arrest of a group of guys who tried to topple a Martin Luther King Jr. statue. Aiden had blown him off that day to drop some acid with Danny Pile. Nix was making up angry texts to Aiden in his head, handing out pamphlets about gender neutral bathrooms and pedophiles, when Emmy approached him, all blond ponytail, white button-up shirt and slim khakis tucked into boots. She was at least ten years older than him, but his body didn't care or know the difference; it was very happy to meet her. Then she'd opened her mouth and his brain caught fire. He'd never met anyone else who was so interested in his ideas. Over coffee with her later that day, he'd told her opinions and convictions he'd never shared with anyone up to then, even Aiden. She encouraged him, drew him out when he lost confidence. He'd felt a little embarrassed when he met Dwight for the first time and the man quoted Nix's words back at him. Nix was disappointed Emmy had told her dad his rambling philosophy but couldn't bring himself to be mad about it; it was what launched him into Dwight's orbit.

Dermot Street was announced through the sound system. The train slowed to a halt. He heard the shuffling of passengers boarding the train and the *ding-ding* of the doors closing. A lot of them, by the sound of it. Not so many that one took a seat next to him. He smiled under his bandana. With his knees splayed in his camouflage pants, arms folded, skull face and cap bib meeting almost to the point of hiding his eyes, he knew they recognized him as an alpha. The low-toned baseball chatter made him think it was a post-game crew. Pretty quiet, though. Their team must've lost. His smile turned to a sneer. Sheeple. Hooked on every distraction - rigged sports, finger-licking fast fat food, megalomedia - while their country was getting stolen out from under them.

Aiden was distracted. Girls for sure, but Nix understood that one. Drugs were the problem. Nix had given up weed a year ago, when he got serious about the movement. Aiden was still at it. They'd been mirror images of each other for so long Nix figured Aiden would follow him by example, if not for his own sake. It didn't happen. It got worse. Weed was still Aiden's day-to-day, but he'd been dipping his toe into coke and pills since Nix started spending more time with the White Lights. That's why he'd pushed to get Aiden to a Lights meeting a couple of weeks ago; the members were basically ascetics. Aiden wasn't serious enough about it yet to join, but Nix knew being in the Lights without him was going to feel like being in the biggest race of his life with one leg broken. He hoped giving Aiden glimpses of the big picture would help his friend drop his blinders. Fast.

The train slowed and a man's voice came over the speaker: "Shelby Cross Station". Nix opened his eyes and looked at the full car of blue-and-orange-dressed passengers. Oversized foam fingers pointed at the floor and metallic streamers hung limply from hands. He smirked under his bandana and walked to the doors. He was the only one getting out of the compartment. He exited onto the south end of the platform and watched as two passengers from the opposite end of the train got out near the north end and bounded up the frozen escalator.

He felt a pinch in his neck and a rush of heat.

He grabbed the spot and caught a glimpse of an enormous broad-shouldered man looking down at him, holding a syringe that looked absurdly small in his meaty fingers. A dark hood was hauled over his head and his body went limp.

When Nix was fifteen, he took a shoulder to the temple in a rugby game. Stone-cold unconscious in a blink. He woke up just as suddenly, seconds later, disoriented but he could stand up under his own steam. This was not that. Waking up from a drug-induced blackout was like clawing his way through layers of cotton stuffing. Sounds were muffled. His fingertips tingled. When he managed to flick his eyes open, he had to shut them again so his retinas didn't combust.

"Turn down the lights, Em. You're going to blind the

kid."

He recognized the gummy twang of the voice. "Dwight?"

"Yeah, it's me, kid. Em's got things toned down. Try that again."

He cracked his lids. The glare was gone. Slowly opening them the rest of the way, Nix gave his eyes time to adjust. Dwight and Emmy were sitting at a wooden table pushed up against one wall, a laptop open between them. The floor lamp next to them was bright enough to light up a blue-tiled room with a bare concrete floor that had a small drain in its centre. Nix was sitting, too; he was on a metal chair near the back wall of the room, opposite what looked like the only door in and out. A sick feeling rose in him and he tried to move his hands. He exhaled hard and chuckled when they lifted, unrestrained, from his sides. As if they'd have him tied up? He rubbed them together to force some heat into them and noticed the blood from earlier, still embedded in his cuticles. He unconsciously picked at it while he tried to figure out what he was doing here.

Initiation into the White Lights was a guarded process. Each step of his had been revealed to him only as he'd needed to know it. He'd get a phone call outlining his next test and would be given a timeframe in which to complete it.

"Prepare and send death threats to the three prominent social justice warriors of your choice. You have one day."

"Create two alias Facebook profiles; launch a Facebook group from each profile; post content to engage users who support The While Lights' mandate and objectives. You have one week."

"Disrupt the protesters removing commemorative statues in Southern Green Park. You have two hours."

When he had been given a job, Nix turned himself over to it. He left work mid-shift, dinner with his room-mates mid-chew, basketball with Aiden mid-shot.

He racked his brain to come up with a reason why they'd drug and hustle him wherever this was. He'd have eagerly come to any location they chose, under his own steam. This was…kidnapping was the only word for it. But each step he'd taken for the Lights so far had been a leap of trust; he was ready to take another one. Besides, Dwight and Emmy being here sparked a small hope in his chest. This was the first face-to-face contact he'd had with either of them since his initiation started; it could be a sign that the end was close.

"How's the head?" Dwight asked. He had his hands folded in his lap, legs crossed. He wore the same black polo, blue jeans, deck sneakers combo Nix always saw him in.

"Fine, I think." Nix stretched out his neck. Still a few cobwebs, but better by the minute.

"Are you nervous?" Emmy asked. She was holding a pen tip down on the table, sliding her fingers down it and, when they reached the bottom, flipping the pen over to start again. Nix wished she'd stop. It was hard enough on an average day around Emmy to keep his crotch in check.

He took a second to think what the right answer was. If he was nervous, would they think he didn't trust them? If he wasn't, would they take that to mean he didn't take them, or the organization, seriously? He settled on telling them yes, he was nervous – about whether he finished the last task to their satisfaction.

"That's why we're here," Emmy said. "We got your video." She clicked a button on the laptop and the screen brightened. An image of Nix's head connecting with the protester's nose was frozen on the screen. She tapped again and the video played. Dwight and Emmy watched the screen; Nix watched them for their reactions. Nothing notable, besides a small compression at the corner of Dwight's mouth when Nix shouted "White Lights! BOOYAH!"

When the video ended, Dwight closed the laptop and sighed. "It was almost perfect." He stood and walked toward Nix, who sat straighter in the chair. "All you had to do was put that guy down and walk away." He got close enough that his knees were almost touching Nix's. Nix had to tip his head back at a painful angle to meet his eyes. "You weren't asked to say our name or publicize it."

Nix's mind raced. Aiden had uploaded it to the dark web site where they posted videos of anything that would get them booted off mainstream websites. Nix hadn't given it a second thought. It wasn't like they put it on Facebook. He scrambled for the right answer. He'd never thrown Aiden under the bus. Ever. Not when they were thirteen and his parents caught him with a stack of *Hustler* Aiden had asked him to hide; not a month ago when Arty had put a baseball bat to Nix's bike because he wouldn't give up where Aiden had stashed Arty's bag of coke. They covered each other's asses. But that was kids' stuff. Nix needed to build a life with the Lights.

"It's too bad. We – I – trusted you. Your judgement.

You had a lot of potential." Emmy said this to him from her seat at the table. She looked at her hand, flipping the pen, shaking her head. "It's my fault, Daddy. I thought… it doesn't matter. I'm sorry."

Dwight continued to stare into Nix's eyes. Every second that passed wound Nix so tight it was as if someone was turning a jack-in-the-box handle between his shoulder blades. Tighter and tighter went the spring. Dwight leaned down and ripped the skull bandana down off his face.

"Why are you wearing that stupid thing? You look like a child's idea of a soldier. Or, are you trying to be a common thug? I thought you understood the work we're doing here."

In the confusion of waking up and facing the two of them, Nix had forgotten he had it on. The knot on the bandana came loose easily under his fingers. He balled it up and dropped it on the floor.

Dwight turned on his heel and strode back to the table. Before his feet stopped, he had the collar of Emmy's blue shirt bunched in his fist.

"Hey! I understand! I do!" Nix was shouting the words, on his feet and a step closer to the table before Dwight rounded on him.

"Put your Goddamn ass in that chair or I'll have Weevil come in and chain you to it."

Nix figured Weevil to be the gorilla who'd jabbed him with the syringe earlier. Strong as he felt, he knew he wasn't up to a battle with King Kong. He sat down, perched on the very edge of the seat, hands flexing between his knees.

"I told you," Dwight said quietly to Emmy's wide-eyed, upturned face. She'd dropped the pen on the table and was holding her father's wrist with both hands. "I told you I was sick of you bringing me stupid, weak, dickless wonders. I told you what would happen if the next one didn't measure up."

"I'm sorry," Emmy choked out on a sob. "He seemed… he's different when he's around the other one…maybe…"

"Maybe what? He'll grow a pair? I won't hold my breath." The last word was delivered with a shake of Emmy's collar before he let her go and ran his hands through his hair and paced the room. Her eyes darted to Nix's. Her mouth opened and closed like she wanted to speak but couldn't find the words. From across the room he could see tears welling in her eyes. In the year since he'd met Dwight, he'd seen him lose it at a Lights member who turned up late with audio gear for a rally, heard him ripping a reporter a new one over the phone, but nothing like this spontaneous rage.

"Dwight. Please. It's not her fault. I'm committed. Totally. I can do better. I'll do better." Nix spilled the words so quickly dribbles of spit beaded on his lips. His eyes were darting between Dwight and Emmy, looking for a sign of changing mood in the room. He might as well be sitting in a compressor. He'd screwed it up. His plans, slipping. And Emmy. What would happen to her? He didn't think Dwight would hurt his own daughter. Would he? He was so *pissed*. "I didn't know." The lie slid out of Nix's mouth like a serpent. "I didn't know he'd uploaded it. Aiden. He did it. I can take it down." Nix's mouth started to water and filled with a sharp sour taste.

"So, it was Aiden's fault?" Dwight stood over him again, flipping Nix's hat off with his hand. Nix grabbed at it, but Dwight snagged him by the chin and forced his attention upward.

"Yes. Aiden." Nix knew in any other place, any other time, he'd be mortified by the tears gathering in his eyes and the snot prickling the edge of his nostrils. Even with Emmy watching, all he could feel was hollow fear. Panic that the White Lights were slipping out of his reach. They got it; they got *him*. He couldn't lose that. His need pushed aside his disgust with himself for lying, blaming Aiden. And wasn't it really Aiden's fault anyway? He'd posted the video. Nix hadn't asked him to do that; he'd been getting ready to take it down, hadn't he? Thought about it at least?

"Okay, Nixon. Okay." Dwight let his chin go and grabbed him by the back of the neck, keeping Nix's face angled up. "What are we going to do about it?"

"I'll take it down. I'll do it myself. I promise I won't make—"

"I don't think that's going to solve it." He let Nix go and walked to the door. He cracked it open and said something Nix couldn't hear. Heavy footsteps clunked down the hallway. A long, slow stride. Dwight stepped back to open the door and Weevil walked in. He held a .38 special; it looked like a kid's toy in his massive hand.

"Oh shit, oh shit. Dwight. Don't. No. I'll do anything. I...want this. The Lights. So much." Nix was out of his chair, standing behind it like it could give him protection. "Emmy?" He glanced at her. She had her elbows on her knees, staring at the floor.

"I know you want this. Nixon, I was so impressed with you. Your ideas. You see the war that's coming. But you're weak." He nodded at Weevil.

"No. No! I can do this, I…" He trailed off when Weevil turned and waved his arm through the open door. The sound of rustling clothes and squeaking footsteps came from the hallway. A tall, heavy-set man with a shaved head dragged a stocky teenager in a camouflage hoodie through the door, hand clamped around the kid's bicep. Nix's eyes scanned the kid's familiar face, taking in the swollen right eye and split lower lip. Tall guy shoved; Aiden stumbled and fell to his knees.

"What did you do to him?" Nix asked Dwight. He squeezed the back of the chair so hard his knuckles strained and popped, but kept the seat between him and the ambiguity in the rest of the room.

"Nix? Man, are you okay?" Aiden's voice was high and thin, like he couldn't get enough air.

"You're weak," Dwight repeated to Nix. "And this is your weakness." He twisted Aiden's hood in his fist, tightening the cloth like a noose. Aiden gurgled and grabbed at his throat, his hood.

"Aiden?" Nix took a step around the chair. Dwight twisted tighter. "Stop! All right! What's he doing here?"

"I'm going to do you a favour, Nixon. Some people can't help being weak. It's in their DNA. They're bred that way. But you're lucky." Dwight dropped Aiden's hood and stepped in a wide circle around his heaving, coughing body. "We can cut yours out."

Nix stared at him, mind racing. Aiden. His weakness?

How? Cut it out?

Dwight nodded his head at Weevil and walked back to Nix. He passed Emmy and bent to whisper in her ear. She nodded and Nix thought he saw her lips curve at the corner through the drape of her hair, but he blinked and it was gone. Emmy stood up and looked over her shoulder at him when she walked across the threshold of the door. She was frowning, eyes wide with worry. She disappeared down the hall without a word. Her smile had to have been an illusion; he was so uneasy his imagination was in overdrive.

Nix's attention was jerked back to the room when Dwight put his hand between Nix's shoulder blades and shoved him toward Aiden, snagging the chair in his other hand. Its metal legs screeched across the bare concrete and joined Aiden's yells to be let go. The cascade of sound had Nix's ears ringing. Aiden was still on his knees, Weevil's broad palm clamped onto the back of his neck and his .38 pressed to Aiden's temple. Dwight slammed the chair down and shoved Nix into it so hard he almost fell off the seat.

"You think he's your friend?" Dwight asked, pointing at Aiden. "Does he support your dreams? Your beliefs?"

"He's...he's been—"

"Why hasn't he joined the Lights? Like you? What did he tell you?"

Weevil ground the .38 into Aiden's skull hard enough to make him yelp. Nix tried to speak, but Dwight got there first.

"He thinks we're too extreme, doesn't he?"

Nix thought about the conversations he'd had with

Aiden about the Lights over the past year. He remembered Aiden using that word more than once. But he always stepped away from it when Nix explained why the Lights had it right, why they needed to be at the brutal edge of the fight to protect what was theirs.

"You don't need to tell me. He said it himself at the meeting you brought him to. Didn't care who he insulted. He told Rose Crawley she was a backwoods hillbilly."

Aiden tried to pull away from Weevil, but the giant's hands didn't budge. "Nix, she told me she wanted to bring back lynch mobs and put people in concentration camps. I get protecting your house, your corner, but that's holocaust level. That's what these people are about. You can't want that."

"Why did you have to say that, Aiden?"

"Because he's the weakness, Nixon. He doesn't understand what's at stake the way you do. The way the Lights do."

"You're a fucking cult!" Aiden shouted and Weevil cracked him on the back of the head with the butt of the pistol. Aiden swayed.

"Dwight, don't. He's scared. He doesn't know what he's saying." Nix folded the material of his pants between his fingers, pinching and smoothing it. Rubbing his palms against his thighs. He had to stop this. Everything was falling apart. A thought shimmied through his confusion. "He helped!" Nix shouted. "Today. He helped me. He tried to get me past my initiation. He gets it!"

"Sure he does." Dwight moved behind Nix and patted him on both shoulders, keeping his hands there. "Why don't you ask him why he helped you today? He was happy to tell us after we encouraged him."

Nix looked at his friend, whose head was bent, hiding his face. Nix thought he was still stunned from the crack Weevil had given him.

"I did it for you. To keep you out of trouble." The words were slurred and seemed pulled from the bottom of Aiden's belly.

Nix felt some tension leave his shoulders at this harmless disclosure. "See? He does stuff like that all the time. I do it for him. He's cool, Dwight. Seriously."

"What else?" Dwight said. When Aiden didn't answer, Dwight's finger flicked on Nix's shoulder and Weevil grabbed Aiden by the chin, holding his face up. Blood had trickled from his temple, across the swollen lower lid of his eye while his head was down. It dripped down his cheek like tears from the corner of his eye. "Tell your friend Nixon what you did."

"Aiden?" A coil of fear wound around his chest.

"You can't see it, Nix." The pressure of Weevil's hand forced Aiden to press the words out through his clenched jaw. "They *recruited* you. They're using you. Ergh!" Nix saw Weevil's hand tighten on Aiden's face. "I put up the video. I did it to get you out." Aiden posted the video on the dark web to get him in trouble with the Lights? That didn't make sense; Nix wanted them to see it. "I don't underst—"

"Enough!" Dwight shouted. Nix jerked sideways in the chair and Dwight grabbed him by the shirt to straighten him up. "This is taking forever. He put the video on YouTube, Nix. He tried to set the cops on you."

"What the…" Nix's heart pounded. He fumbled in his

pocket for his phone, thumbed the YouTube app. He tried two, three searches to turn up the video, but got random hits from the protest. Nothing with him in it. His pulse took a slower turn. "It's not. Was it? Did you do that?" Aiden didn't respond.

"It wasn't up for long," Dwight said. "We caught it because we were monitoring the news and social media today for content about the protest. Aiden was kind enough to use hashtags we follow. By now moderators have taken it down and notified the authorities. That's what your friend did for you."

"Nix, I was trying to help." Aiden worked every word through a foam of spittle and blood on his lips. "Out of control, man. Wouldn't listen to me…maybe if you got a scare, faced the fallout, you'd see. Get away from them… I'm sorry, man. I'm sorry." Real tears mixed with the crimson drops on his cheek.

Nix froze inside. The betrayal was cosmic. Aiden. Trying to get him busted. *For his own good.*

"Helping you? He's jealous of you." Dwight leaned down to speak in Nix's ear. They were both looking at Aiden, whose head was pulled back so far by the pressure of Weevil's hand, his back was bowed. "You've worked so hard, Nixon. You saw the rot in the world and you decided to do something about it. You found us. You found meaning. What does he have? Nothing. And he tried to take everything you've built away from you so you'd have nothing, too. He'd have you in that hole with him. Do friends do that to each other, Weevil?"

King Kong didn't move or make a sound.

"You put your trust in him. It made you weak. Exposed." Dwight's words were warm against his ear. They were thawing Nix's cold disbelief. Stoking it to something that stung and scorched. "White Lights can't have vulnerabilities. Right now, you're a vulnerability, Nixon."

It burned bright. Hot. The feeling inside him. Aiden had tried to take it all from him. He'd pretended to be his friend. Today. Yesterday, when they got burgers and made plans for the protest. How long had Aiden been faking it? Two weeks ago, when Nix had taken him to the Lights meeting?

"Why did you go to that Lights meeting?" Nix asked, eyes boring into Aiden's.

"Trying to help you." Barely above a whisper. Weak.

"He spent his time watching. Pumping people for information." Dwight straightened and clenched Nix's shoulders so hard he jumped. "What did he do with it? The police are very interested in us. Maybe he passed it on to them."

"Didn't." Aiden got one shake of his head in before Weevil clamped down and kept him still. "Learning. For you."

Fury. That's what this was. Nix'd felt it this afternoon, when that idiot, loudmouth protester waved his *WHY IS ENDING RACISM A DEBATE?* sign, shouting, "Fascist!" into Nix's face. Rage. Sweat broke out across his forehead. It trickled down the dent of his spine and into the waistband of his pants. Aiden was trying to take him away from the Lights. From Dwight. Emmy. Just like the degenerates who were trying to take away everything his people had fought for and earned; just like the government who was handing it over to them.

"No, you're worse than them," Nix said, voice shaking. Aiden was worse than all the other enemies because he'd pretended to be his friend.

Aiden's eyes flickered. He started panting. Nix picked up a pungent scent of sweat and wondered if it was him or Aiden.

"Trying to carve you out of—" That was as far as Aiden got before Weevil squeezed off the air in his throat.

"I told you I could cut out your weakness." Dwight came around in front of Nix, blocking his view of Aiden. His voice got louder, tone sharper. "Is that what you want?"

Nix stared at Dwight's belt buckle: a thick pewter oval with the country's flag waving above the words, "*COME AND TAKE IT*". Nix remembered the night Dwight had shown him the tiny knife that slid out from behind the buckle. "Haven't had to use it. Yet." He'd said it matter-of-factly, as if to slip it between someone's ribs wouldn't bother him. Dwight wasn't weak. He was impregnable. Brilliant. Nix's breath came fast and shallow. His head spun. Aiden. Undermining him. Rejecting him. No different than his parents.

Weak.

"If we don't cut it out, it will kill your purpose. The White Lights will be over for you." Dwight's rally voice filled the room, ringing off the walls.

Gone. All of it. Because of Aiden. His brother in every way that mattered.

Dwight dropped his volume again, spoke gently. "We'll take care of it. You don't have to say a word."

Aiden's muffled shouts drowned out Dwight's next

words. A thick sound of meat hitting meat and the muffled shouting turned to a quiet sob.

"But if you tell me not to, you and Aiden can leave. You'll never hear from me or the Lights again. You can have your old life back. I'll give you a couple of days to find a new job, a new place to live."

Nix raised his head to Dwight. The look in the man's eyes told him what Dwight saw when he looked at Nix wasn't a peer, but a kid - jaw clenched tight, tears pricking his eyes. Nix grabbed the cool metal of the chair seat, dug the hard edge into his fingers until they stung. He stared at Dwight without blinking, willing the tears back, letting the muscles in his face change, soften. He raised his chin.

A shuffle and grunt behind Dwight and Aiden's voice, "They're taking you away from everyone, Nix. Don't listen. They're going to get you kil—"

"Weevil?" Dwight interrupted.

The gunshot exploded on the heels of the giant's name.

Nix hiccupped and hot bile raced into his mouth. His restrained retching and spitting were the only sounds. A potent stink of urine filled the room. He shifted in his seat. Thank God, all dry. Nix wasn't sure if it was seconds or minutes that passed between the shot and the deep thump of something heavy falling to the floor. He did know it was exactly twenty-six heartbeats later that he heard moaning and the scratch of zippers and boots and fingers scraping across the concrete.

Dwight tilted his head and kept his narrowed eyes on Nix. It felt to Nix as if everything he'd worked for, everything he wanted, relied on him keeping his eyes fixed on the man standing above him. Nix beat back the dark, heavy sensation trying to wrap itself around his heart, fearful it would make his eyes restless. Even when a crawling form came into his peripheral vision, he didn't look away. He maintained his line of sight when the form stood up and leaned against the wall with one hand to keep upright. Nix didn't falter when the form said, "You. Fuck you, man. You deserve them." He kept his gaze straight and steady on Dwight's when the form shuffled through the open door with Weevil in tow.

Nix's lungs burned. When had he taken a breath last?

Dwight stuck out his hand. Nix sucked in air and grabbed the man's forearm, pulling himself to his feet. His knees gave out. Dwight held him up. Nix expected a sneer for this sign of fragility, but the man stayed quiet with his hand on Nix's elbow. Was he waiting for Nix to say something? What could he say after watching the man pretend to kill his best friend? No, his betraying, son-of-a-bitch former friend, he reminded himself.

"I'm sorry I doubted your commitment," Dwight eventually offered, pulling his hand back from Nix's arm. "I wasn't sure you had it in you. You're one of the strongest people I've met."

Nix's chest puffed out. The purity of pleasure that coursed through him at Dwight's compliment left him every bit as lightheaded as he'd been the moment Weevil pulled the trigger.

The gun.

"Blanks?" Nix asked.

Dwight nodded and put his arm around Nix's shoulder. "We're not monsters."

Nix thought about telling Dwight he was glad Aiden was alive, that he wondered what would happen the next time he saw him on the M train. With his temper cooled, he realized having him gone from his life was going to be bad enough; he didn't want him gone from the planet. But he didn't say any of those things. Instead, as they walked out into the hallway, he asked, "I guess you're going to go find Emmy?"

"Emmy? Why?"

"You gave her a good fright, Dwight. You should talk to her."

He frowned and pursed his lips. "Fright?"

Dwight was pretty angry when he went at Emmy. Maybe he was blanking on grabbing her by the shirt. Nix reminded him.

"Of course! Right." He cleared his throat. "Yes, apologize. I'll do that." He walked a few steps, arm still around Nix's shoulders. "You like Emmy, don't you?" Nix imagined his fingers tangled in her long smooth hair, kissing her lips. Heat rose to his cheeks and other parts lower down. Dwight chuckled. "I'd never have guessed."

3

Jad breathed deep and closed his eyes while Sasha rubbed between his shoulder blades. "Gonna keep it down this time, big fella?" she asked. He nodded slowly, a dash of colour trying to push its way up through his grey skin. "I told you to take Gravol before we came. I don't know how a guy who can't play most video games thought he could do an immersive sim and not trigger his motion sickness."

"Is anyone else getting these after-effects?" Scott asked. "Last time it was the tightness in my throat. This time I smell sweat and pee."

Jad urged.

"Me too," Sasha said. "Not much, but it's there."

"The Virtoken does stimulate sensory areas of the brain, to enhance your experience," Cinn said. "It happens to a different degree in every guest during the simulation. Any post-simulation sensations are psychosomatic."

"Feels real to me," Scott muttered.

"Exactly," Cinn said. "Psychosomatic. I took for granted that you knew the definition."

"So," Jad piped up after a couple of swallows, "whose

grave is it?"

"Nixon's, obviously," Scott said.

"Aiden's," Sasha said at the same time.

Four heads turned toward Percivet Cinn.

"I cannot say," he replied.

A chorus of "C'mon man", "That's not fair", and other rejections of his answer echoed between the stones.

"Why do you think it's Nixon?" Sasha asked Scott.

"He was clearly on his way to a bad end, caught up with that bunch of fascists. I'd say he came up against someone nastier than him and took a bullet."

"Or, Aiden stayed with the drugs and got himself into trouble or O.D.'d," Sasha shot back.

"And what, Nixon came all the way out here to dress down his old friend's tombstone?" Scott asked. "He didn't seem like that kind of guy."

"If Aiden did it, he'd have a lot more to say about Nixon than 'LOST SOUL' after the guy gave the okay for him to be shot in the face," Sasha said.

"Why do you guys think either of them was responsible for this?" Jad added, pointing to the altered gravestone. "A drunk hobo could've done it. Any rando."

"Hey!" Kinna raised her voice above the three of theirs. "Why do you even think that story was real?" She pointed at Cinn. "He said the stories can be interpretations. If Aiden and Nixon fell out, it was probably just a fight. Nobody would do that to his best friend in real life. Right?" The latter question was addressed to Cinn.

"Your faith in humanity is delightful," he said. His grin revealed his flawless blue teeth. "People have been called to action by far less powerful motivators than the sense of belonging or abandonment. But you are correct; the friendship could have ended in any number of ways."

"Can you at least tell us if there's such a thing as the White Lights?" Kinna asked.

"There is," Scott jumped in, waving his phone in Kinna's direction. "They're a white supremacist organization." His finger slid up the screen. "And…yep, Dwight King was the founder. Has a daughter Emily. Good job on the details, Cinn."

"Weren't those the tiki-torch jokers from the protest a few years ago?" Jad asked.

"I don't think so. These guys are more hardcore. They're implicated in some church and synagogue bombings, shootings." Scott clicked the sleep button and put the phone back in his pocket. "No mention of a Nixon or an Aiden."

"Cannon fodder," Kinna mumbled.

"Come children." Cinn turned his back to them and began walking back up the path.

"Dude, not a child," Jad said. "I'll be eighteen in a few months."

He slipped his phone out of Sasha's hand and kept it angled to allow the projection to move forward.

"That will no longer be necessary, Mr. Erim," Cinn said. "Your Virtokens have adapted to the visual and auditory functions in your brain. I can now interact with you synaptically, independent of projection. Simply keep your phone active on the Cramon Cemetery application and it will communicate with the Virtoken to provide the data for our tour."

Jad frowned, but hit the sleep button on the phone.

For an instant, Kinna saw two Cinns walking ahead of her, a second out of sync: four arms, four legs, two heads. A brief glitch in the tech, but in this place, enough to give her a quick chill up her spine. He resolved to a single shape, this one more dynamic. His glowing blue form had gone 3D.

Scott was rubbing the disc on the back of his neck like it might explode. Jad paused to lean on a low, narrow headstone and closed his eyes, skin dewy.

"Holy crap, this tech is amazing," Sasha said.

Kinna nodded, but her feelings about having Percivet Cinn rattling around her brain sat somewhere between Sasha's thrill and Scott's obvious discomfort. *He's in the disc, Kinna, not your head.* Besides, she reminded herself, it's not so different than the next gen Neuralink that launched a couple of years ago for the holographic home assistant. It's good. It's all good.

"...super tense, but a palate cleanser." Kinna tuned back in mid-way through Sasha and Scott's conversation.

"Yeah," Scott said. "That cat thing gave me the heebie-jeebies. Guns and fists and people being miserable to each other - that's my comfort zone. Even though, you know, the smell."

"Then you will be pleased with our next offering, Mr. Mahoney," Cinn said without turning.

"What've you got for us, Percy?" Jad called out, trotting up from behind and throwing his arms over Sasha's and Scott's shoulders. His complexion had lost the thin sheen of sweat and his smile was wide.

Cinn glanced at Jad. Kinna thought she saw their host frown before his photons reorganized back into pleasant perfection. He waved his hand and the map opened again. Their red dot was almost on top of another spinning star. This one sat in a more jumbled area of the cemetery than their last stop. She shone her light in the direction of the next marker. The beam skid across an area spiked with obelisk-style headstones. The words engraved on some of the stones nearest to them were suggested by their shadows, but too faint to read. A rectangular mausoleum about the size of two phone booths loomed over the markers. The fog swirled and was thinner here. Not enough to offer deep views into the cemetery, but enough for Kinna to make out stubby human shapes leaning against the four pillars at the corners of the tomb and the pointed roof of green weathered bronze they supported. The shapes appeared to be shifting. Kinna squinted her eyes for a better look, figuring (hoping) the curling mist was creating an illusion of movement.

The map evaporated and Cinn took a path of cobbled stones that ended at the foot of the mausoleum. Kinna felt her shoulders relax when she realized her mystery shapes were four carved, perfectly still, winged cherubs. One held an hourglass, another a skull. The third cradled a raven in its arms and the last one held up balance scales. A door stained the same green as the roof was set between two of the pillars. CROSBIE was carved into the lintel above the tomb's entrance.

"Do the names Shackleton, Franklin, and Amundsen mean anything to you children?" Cinn asked.

"Stop with the kid thing, would you?" Jad huffed.

"Yeah, polar explorers," Sasha said.

Cinn tipped his head in her direction. "Famous for

their expeditions to the Arctic and Antarctic, as often due to their successes as their failures. And Crosbie? Have you heard this name in relation to polar exploration?"

They shook their heads or shrugged in response.

He walked around the side of the mausoleum. The wall of the building was carved with names and dates, each enclosed in a rectangular border, some plain, others with decorative scrolling at the edges. Kinna and Scott read them out in turn.

"Jane G. Crosbie. February 15, 1853 to February 1, 1906."

"William Crosbie. August 5, 1876 to January 20, 1950."

"Private Lance P. Crosbie. October 14, 1894 – July 1, 1916."

"Vice-admiral Alphonsus B. Crosbie," Cinn added. "November 7, 1829 to September 16, 1931."

"Over a hundred years old!" Scott said. "What a tough old bastard."

"Indeed. Vice-admiral Crosbie was an adventurous and successful navy man. He was decorated for bravery in multiple military campaigns. When he retired, he settled on a family estate inherited from a distant relative and donated most of the produce and meat he farmed to the poor. It was said he would share food from his own plate rather than see a person go hungry.

Most importantly, he was the lone survivor of Franklin's ill-fated voyage to find a route through the Northwest Passage. The only man out of a crew of 129 to make it out of the Arctic. Despite all of this, he is virtually unknown."

"I've never heard his name," Kinna said.

"Me either," Scott said.

Cinn blinked at them. "As I said, he is virtually unknown."

"Don't have to be snarky about it, Percy," Jad said.

Cinn turned his head in Jad's direction. "I do not 'snark'. May I continue?"

"Is it just me, or is he getting an attitude," Sasha whispered to Kinna as Cinn picked up his narrative.

"Franklin is more famous for dying in the Arctic than Crosbie is for surviving. We are lucky he left a record of his experiences in journals and letters. From these, and a few necessary deductions, we have prepared a story I think will leave you chilled, in more ways than one."

WHAT WE BECOME
ON THE ICE

When Pitt suggests we draw lots, my mouth waters for the first time in days. Not with joyful hope for a plate of food, but as a lubricant for the vomit my body wants to eject. It doesn't understand there's nothing there to throw up, not even a pitiful mouthful of bile.

"John 15:13," Pitt says. *"Greater love has no one than this, that someone lay down his life for his friends."*

His words take me back to Sunday school, Father O'Byrne snapping the pointer at the blackboard to drive home the moral lesson of whichever bible verse he'd scrawled there. It feels like a hundred years since I sat in the small room at the back of the church with Nance and Molly and the others, smelling the chalk dust and hearing the tick of coal burning in the stove. To see me, you'd think I'd *lived* a hundred years since then as well, instead of the three that have passed in reality. Back then, my face was soft and smooth, close to needing its first shave. My mother wouldn't recognize me with this beard I've got now, scraggly thing it is. Any skin not covered by it is peeling, red and raw, stretched thin across the ridges of bone at my cheeks and eyes. I haven't seen a mirror in a year or more, but I look at Pitt and Davis, glance at the pile of rags near the tent flaps (Banfield), and know I must be as chapped and bony as them.

My fingers and toes, that's another story. I can see them just fine. Except the half-dozen I'm missing. Black had crept in at the tips and edges until they became something like the nubs of coal I used to drop into the school stove. Every time the crew held me down to cut one off, I'd wonder whether the little things would burn like coal, too.

I lost the last one about six months ago, when it was dead of winter, almost full dark. Back then, there must've been fifty of us, still huddled in the shadow of our ice-bound vessel, wrapped up in what was left of her sails. Frosted ropes clung to her canted masts like sinew on bone. One of the old timers, believe he was an engineer, got the devil in him one night and started pointing at it, saying it was a hand, the leviathan come, breaking through the ice to take us. With liquid fire scorching the oozing stub where my finger used to be, the hollow rot in my guts, and the boys getting squirrelly, I wished that night the fella had been right; I'd have been grateful for the end.

But Davis came through the next day with our first fresh food in weeks: dark, slippery seal meat from a small cow he'd shot. It was a feast for those of us who could keep the rubbery, fishy mess down. Brought us back to the reality that our ship, *Erebus*, was nothing but a broken hulk - a wooden memorial to the souls the ice had already claimed. Her ribs were cracked below the waterline, waiting for the ice to thaw and the ocean to finally take her.

"Crosbie, are you listening?"

I shake free of the memories and look into Pitt's barren eyes.

"Draw lots," I say. He nods, his crown of rags dipping down to the bridge of his nose. "The way we drew lots for the shotgun?" I ask. He doesn't move, but Davis shifts under the spotted grey seal pelt slung over his shoulders, the thing so blasted by ice and snow it looks like a swarm of moths have been at it. Banfield contributes more of the whining moan he took up last night.

"I thought we moved on from that, lad," Pitt says.

"Don't call me lad. You're only a year older than me, and half the man, at that." His lips tighten and I squash the urge to bare my yellowed teeth. "And yes, we settled it. Doesn't mean I forget who I'm dealing with."

Pitt unslings the shotgun and tosses it on the tangle of cloth that serves as the floor of our tent. It lands within arm's reach of where I'm sitting.

"Here. Have it."

We ran out of shot and powder two weeks ago. Pitt kept it anyway. It was a good bludgeon, better than anything we'd find out on the snowscape, in case the bears came again or anyone got out of line. Him handing it over to me is a message: the power is shifting from the gun to something else. Or he wants me to think it is. Me and Davis share a glance. He shrugs. The man used to be built like a steamer trunk. Two of me could stand in his shadow. When we started out, he could carry a barrel of rum up the gangplank on each shoulder. Now he's the size the rest of us were when we were healthy.

I pick up the gun, my eyes on Pitt's. I haven't handled it since I used it to cave in Lieutenant Fairholme's head.

The lieutenant had been the last officer among us. His fever and hallucinations had gotten so bad he was giving orders that would've sent us all straight to the grave. A third of the crew meant to follow them! That's when I understood rank could no longer measure a man's worth out here.

By that time, the sickness had been ripping through the camp for weeks. We couldn't figure it out at first. The men were hungry, of course, but not starving. Thanks to the rationing, we still had stores of the tinned food we'd been eating for two years or more. The illness started with one of the able seamen. He was found cutting himself on the legs and arms, crying about his wife. He broke wild if you went near them. By the time his sores started appearing there were already a dozen others showing signs. They mostly curled into tent corners, shrieking about their tormented joints. I found one man creeping around the camp on his hands and knees, a trickle of blood staining the snow behind him. He'd scratched at the icy surface until his fingertips bled. He told me if he could just dig far enough, he'd get back to Aberdeen, where his father lived.

The surgeon said it was infection from cuts and bad teeth, but wander around the camp and you heard men praying for Jesus to expel whatever demon was running loose among them or for God to help them escape. I imagine that's why some of them bought into the lieutenant's insane ramblings.

Crushing the man's skull was dirty work. The blood and gore froze instantly to the butt of the gun and it was only by scraping it off with an ulu — a curved blade traded to us by the Inuit during our first winter — that it came clean. I wished later that I'd used my knife to do him. But in the moment, when I stood over the lieutenant in his tent, knowing he was going to get us all killed if he didn't stop talking, I couldn't take my eyes off the shotgun laying next to him. I didn't know it was in my hand until I was burying it in his head shouting, "STOP! STOP! STOP!"

Of course, a bullet would've been cleanest, but our supply of shot and powder was already dwindling.

Not to say the men didn't have their clans before, but with the last officer gone, a gulf opened between us. Only twelve crew left by then and half of them looked to me to lead them. Me! A seventeen-year-old on his first sea voyage who drifted to sleep wondering if he'd ever see his mother again. But the new measure of leadership on the ice was strength and decisiveness, and the older men were either too sick or too confounded by our situation to want to be in charge.

And I had the shotgun.

I'd have led them, too, despite the fear that coiled in my belly at the idea of it, except Pitt came up with the idea to draw lots.

The memory of what happened is as crisp and searing as the wind howling outside our tent. I force it away. My concentration isn't what it used to be. I haven't eaten in four days. In the beginning I could last for two or more weeks without food, but my body has so little left to give. I need all my focus to figure out how Pitt is planning to make sure he's on the surviving end of the contest he's proposing.

He stands over me and watches me turn the shotgun over in my hands, run what's left of my fingers over the notched and scored butt. I try to pull back both hammers, but they're seized.

"Why draw lots?" I ask him, hitching my thumb at our moaning crewman curled on the tent floor. "Could just be Banfield."

"With those sores all over him?" Davis says. "I wouldn't touch him to wipe my arse on his coat, let alone—"

"Should be you anyway, Pitt," I say. "What do you think, Davis? It's his fault we've only got this far, with summer almost over. If we'd left *Erebus* when I said, we'd be at Back River, maybe on our way to the Hudson Bay outpost. But we're stuck, starving in this canvas crypt." I wave my arm around to take in the tent, the four of us, our condition, then point at Pitt. "He got himself in charge and put it in your heads that the rescue party was coming. That they'd arrive before we starved." I lay the gun across my knees and lean on it. "If the bears hadn't started stalking the camp, we'd probably all still be there. And now? Everyone else is gone and we're left drawing lots to live?" I shake my head and stare at Pitt. "You were scared to leave that ship, is all. I hope you feel the guilt right down to the soles of your feet."

Every word tightens the lines around Pitt's cadaverous eyes.

It's personal for me, not only principle. Goddamn Pitt. Because of him, I almost met my end.

Early in the spring, after I'd exhausted myself trying to convince him and the men it was a death sentence to stay with the ship, I drew into myself. One evening, I sat shivering next to the fire – one of our last – and stared into the darkness. It set its hook in me, tugged me toward the hypothermic surrender beyond the firelight. My heart galloped in my constricted chest. *Stand up and walk.* I heard the words clear as if they'd been whispered in my ear. It will be over. *No hunger. No sickness. Your family thinks you're dead. They've grieved. Let it be over.* The urge to obey the voice was as powerful as any I'd had in my adolescent life to touch a lady's fine, pale ankle. But my fear of dying alone, giving into this place, was primal and complete; it kept me huddled with my companions.

A small raspy voice intrudes on the charged silence following my condemnation of Pitt's leadership.

"You came."

Our heads swivel toward Banfield. I can't remember the last time he spoke.

"Charlotte…"

He rolls onto his stomach, feet pedalling as if climbing a ladder.

"No. Come back."

His fingers claw at the ground and his legs pump faster. His clothes tangle and twist.

"Charlotte!"

Banfield launches to his feet and lurches out the tent flap onto the tundra. Pitt holds the flap open. Overcast sky meets a ridged terrain of snow finer than sand, drifted and kicked up into billowing sails by a wind cold enough to blacken a man's skin. It is white without end. We watch Banfield stagger through the snow, the low-slung sun casting his long shadow in front of him. Neither of us makes a move to go after him. I cross myself and say a silent prayer that the man finds his fiancé, Charlotte, out there on the ice. Pitt lets the flap drop.

I catch Davis blessing himself out of the corner of my eye. His peeling lips move around silent words. He closes with another blessing and sighs. "Lots," he says. "Look, I know we done dirty by you before. Can't change that now. But we'll do it right this time." He looks at Pitt. "We'll do it right."

His words draw me to the past. I cannot fight it. Back to the lee of the *Erebus*.

Pitt called for us to draw lots to decide who would lead us. We gathered up the ribs from the last seal we caught, the bones pink and grizzled, and Banfield used his hatchet to cut all but one of them to equal lengths of four inches. One was cut to three. Parker, let his soul rot, was sickest back then. We all agreed he couldn't handle the responsibility of leading, so he was made the keeper of the bones, driving each of them into the snow so they all looked of equal length. We approached one by one, each taking a bone until everyone had one, and brought them together to compare lengths. Pitt wound up with the short bone. He became our leader and, thus, the holder of the gun.

I was flooded with a desire to bury my fist in the man's face. The feeling left as quickly as it came and into the void slipped the deepest sense of loss I had ever known. I'm ashamed to say I cried, the way I used to as a child when the thunder would shake the window in my bedroom. I cried for myself, for Lieutenant Fairholme, for every man that had been taken by this accursed place. Pitt never made a sound, but through my stinging tears I could see the curl of his lips. *Feeble.* He may as well have said it out loud.

It wasn't until we'd set off for Back River and Parker was at his end, recounting his sins to God for all to hear, that I learned Pitt had promised him an extra portion of meat in exchange for knowing which rib to pick. When I called for justice, when I reminded the remaining men he'd cheated them as well, reminded them he'd yet to bring in a seal, but wouldn't let the better hunters like Davis use the gun, Pitt levelled the loaded shotgun at my belly and asked how I'd like it if he put me on the menu instead. Davis, Banfield and the rest stared at their feet until I retreated to the tent.

I always took Davis to be a simple, but honourable man. His assurance that we will fairly draw the lots this time gives me hope that, whatever the outcome, he is willing to do the right thing.

"All right," I say. "Let's draw. Short one's the loser this time."

Pitt tosses aside his mittens and digs under the tattered flaps of his seal skin. The bones are bare and worn smooth, not pink and grisly, but I recognize them.

"You took them with you?" I ask. "Of all the supplies you could've carried out of that camp, you took those?"

"They're my good luck charms," he says, dropping some on the ground and shaking the three he kept, making the bones click together.

A flash of memory sweeps me. Sitting by the fireplace in our tiny home in Falstone with my sister Molly. Holding a cup of stiff leather and shaking it so the dice inside clack against each other, like the bones, and thud softly against the sides. Dumping them onto the wooden backgammon board. Molly, too young to learn, but me teaching her anyway. Leaving a small piece of myself with her before I set off to sea. Firelight painting a rosy glow on her cheeks. Giving up and collapsing in laughter with her after she grabbed the small round beach rocks we used for pieces and randomly danced them across the board.

The recollection is joy. The warm colourful bloom of it rises through my body, so foreign it's frightening. Everything has been fear, anger and desperation for so long. My old life is a distant vision, washed out by the sterile prison I've been in these past three years. What I wouldn't do to have it back again!

Pitt watches me, tilts his head. A slow smile curves his blackening lips. A rough sore at the corner splits and a small trickle of blood appears.

"How are we going to do this?" Davis asks. "I can hold them, you two can draw."

"Hell with that," I say. "Give them to me."

Pitt looks at Davis, who nods, then his empty eyes

are back on me. He strokes the bones with his fingers, not breaking eye contact. "You hold them, we draw. Is that the idea?"

I unwrap my hand, the one with four fingers left, and hold it out to him. He lays the bones across my palm. Our skin connects. A cold chill slithers up my arm and spreads across my back. I know in that instant I will not win this draw. If Pitt has his way, the life I glimpsed seconds ago will never be mine again. I've faced death every day for years, but the weight of this knowledge releases a terror in me I've felt only once before: that night I almost walked into the darkness. The voice that calls me this time, though, is my mother's, repeating her final words to me as I left home: "No matter what happens, how it goes, you go on like a man. If you face your maker, do it with a straight back and your chin up."

I sit tall and suck in a breath of frigid air. I arrange the bones in my ruined hand, under the flap of my wrap. Even I don't know which is which when I hold them out to Davis and Pitt. Davis leans in and pulls one from my fist. He shuts his hand around it. Pitt bends down, closes his fingertips around a bone. He looks me in the eye and I feel it wiggle in my hand. He makes a thoughtful sound in the back of his throat, then switches to the other bone and pulls it free. Our eyes are still locked as he asks Davis to hold out his hand.

Their bones are the same length.

"Be damned, Crosbie," Pitt says. "Drawing lots doesn't favour you. I'm sorry, lad. I really am."

I open my fist and stare down at the bone. It feels heavy. I rub my fingers the length of it, getting to know the object deciding my fate. One tip is narrow, the other flared and rounded. On both ends, delicate notches all but invisible to the eye, only detectable by feel under the pressure of bare skin.

"So, how do we do this?" I ask. "You going to slit my throat, Pitt?" I toss him the shotgun and he fumbles to catch it. "Or crack me in the head with that?"

"I thought you'd do the honourable thing and walk out there a ways, have a sit down in the snow. You'll fall asleep. You won't even know it's happening. Might be you'll find Banfield out there, keep each other company." He laughs. When Davis doesn't join him, he sighs. "Stay close to the tent, if you like. That way it's easier to find you after, especially if we have to dig for you a bit."

"Hard to carve me up if I'm frozen like that."

Davis looks away, but Pitt is beyond shame. "We'll get you right at the sweet spot. Not too hard, not too soft." He sees my fists clench, the stiffening of my shoulders. "Now, now." He holds the gun in front of him like a crutch. "All's fair. It had to be one of us. It was the only way to give two of us a chance to get out."

Standing up has never been so difficult. I close my eyes when my feet are under me, steadying myself. They flutter open when Davis speaks. "I'm sorry, Crosbie. I wish... well, doesn't matter now. Fair and square this time." I nod. I believe him. He kept the wrappings on his hands when he picked his lot. I believe he doesn't know Pitt's trick of tickling the ends of the bones with his fingers to find the notches on the shortest rib.

At the tent flap, I stop. Pitt moves behind me. I know he wants to put that shotgun on my back and shove me out into the white death, like a herder ushering his sheep to the slaughterhouse. I open the flap and scan the horizon, not knowing I'm looking for Banfield until his absence resonates. Only three of us left. Soon to be two.

"Pitt, would you tell my father something for me if you see him?"

I sense Pitt's hesitation and turn around.

"Tell him I sent you to him, so there'd be a bigger bastard than him in hell." Pitt doesn't have time to bring up the shotgun to defend himself. It gets pinned between our bellies when I throw my weight at him and thrust my right hand into his Adam's apple, burying the rib bone in his throat. My hand feels warm for the first time since I can remember as his hot blood gushes around the bone and through its hollow centre. The wide-open surprise in Pitt's expression is unmistakable. He gurgles on the fluid clogging his airway. I yank the bone out and the red fluid spurts around his fingers and hand as he tries to hold it back. I wrench the shotgun out of his other hand and round on Davis. The man is sitting in the same place, watching but still.

Pitt's knees buckle and he slumps to the floor. Quick puffs of crystalized breath push past his lips. He coughs. Blood bubbles out the corners of his mouth. He shifts his eyes to me. I've seen dozens of men die here, but not like this. There is no familiar brush of scurvy or dysentery. No sign of the sickness that dragged crewmen through a torment of pain and madness before leaving them to bleed out or wander onto the ice. With those men, death could be seen coming: a shadow floating through our small community, whose visit started to feel welcome when it ended a man's suffering. Even when I killed the lieutenant, he was emaciated, paralyzed, lying in a puddle of his own feces. I knew he would've asked for death if he'd been lucid.

It's different with Pitt. Sudden. Avoidable.

His head lies in a halo of freezing blood, the taut flesh of his face touched by cool blue frost. I hold his gaze until it goes blank and the choking stops. Davis watches me take Pitt by the wrists and drag him through the tent opening. I tug, what's left of my strength not enough to get him past the threshold. The air will suck the moisture from my skin if I stay out too long. Then Davis is next to me, taking one wrist and the two of us drag the body into the curve of a large drift behind the tent.

We stumble back inside and lay down, breath coming in gulping heaves, lungs burning from cold and exhaustion. When I can speak, I mumble the verse that's been running through my mind, *"But the one who endures to the end will be saved."*

"Matthew 24:13. I used to think that meant to keep going until someone comes to save you, not that enduring means you're saving yourself."

I snort. "I used to think that, too."

Davis is quiet for so long, I think he has fallen asleep, until he says quietly, "Psalm 86:5."

"For you, O Lord, are good and forgiving, abounding in steadfast love to all who call upon you."

"Do you think God will forgive us?" Davis asks.

"I hope so."

I hope there's room for redemption in this wasteland; forgiveness for what we have become on the ice. I pray for it while I contemplate what comes next.

"How long do we have to leave him out there before we start cutting?" I ask Davis.

"It'll be hard to get anything off him if we let him go solid. I'd say an hour at most."

"Thighs and backside first?"

He nods. "Wasn't much meat on him anywhere. We'll get what we get."

"Nothing left to do, then, but wait," I say, staring up at the peak of the tent.

4

"Amen, hallelujah, praise be, they ate the jackass!"

"You are feeling better this time, Mr. Erim. Excellent."

"Sure am, Percy. That story was delicious."

"For Godsakes, Jad," Sasha said.

"What? Did my joke leave a bad taste in your mouth?"

Sasha rolled her eyes. "Is anyone else cold? I'm shaking here." Jad unzipped his jacket and tucked her inside it, wrapping his arms around her.

"Yeah," Scott said. "I'm freezing. And my mouth tastes like copper." He rubbed his hands together and breathed into them. "More psychosomatics, Cinn? Maybe your tokens need recalibrating."

"I assure you, your Virtokens are working to design specifications," Cinn replied, the fine lines of his face squiggling for an instant. His voice was a touch louder than his usual drawl, Kinna noticed. She flicked her eyes to Scott, Sasha and Jad, looking for any sign they'd noticed the same thing. Nothing. Scott's head was down and, annoyingly, Jad and Sasha were kissing. Kinna started to tell them to get a room but shut her mouth when a spot under her jawline flared in pain. Very specific, like someone was poking her in the throat. Or the muted feeling of being stabbed with a bone shard? She shivered. It was her first side-effect from the simulation. The sensation pulled her straight back into the story, stamping her brain with impressions of pooling blood and amputated fingers. Her cheeks started to tingle and burn. Frostbite?

She flicked on her phone and keyed a search in her browser: Cramon Cemetery Simulation After Effects. As she scrolled the results, she heard Scott say, "I find it hard to believe a decorated war hero admitted to cannibalism. Is that one of those bits you 'interpreted'?"

"That is for you to decide, Mr. Mahoney," Cinn replied. Kinna glanced up. His face and tone were immaculately rendered and utterly pleasant. She went back to her search.

"It says here they found evidence of lead poisoning in the bodies and skeletons they turned up from the Franklin expedition over the years," Sasha said. She'd come up for air and had her phone wedged between hers and Jad's bodies. "Hang on. My signal is dropping." She raised the phone in the air and waved it around. "Okay, here. A bunch of them had scurvy, too. That would explain how they all got sick and went crazy."

"It *could*, yes," Cinn said.

"Some of the skeletons had knife marks on them, too. Several bones cracked open to…" She trailed off and wrinkled her nose.

Scott motioned with his hand for her to continue.

"Well, this is what a Smithsonian website says: *'When*

it happens out of necessity, cannibalism occurs in phases. First, people cut flesh from bones, focusing on big muscle groups. When things get even direr, they start to break the bones apart to get at the fat-rich marrow inside. This is called end-stage cannibalism, and it's usually part of a last-ditch effort to survive.' "

She put the phone away and looked at Crosbie's name on the mausoleum wall. "This guy did that?"

"All that time he spent later in his life making sure people didn't go hungry," Scott said. "Compensating for something?"

Kinna's signal was dropping in and out, too, but she'd been able to click a dozen links before the stupid browser got too slow to bother with. None of the results she'd read talked about after-effects from the Virtokens. A couple mentioned the psychosomatic explanation. Kinna sighed, which led into a massive yawn. The intensity of the stories was taking a toll on all of them; no wonder their senses were amped up, on edge.

Cinn unfurled his map again. He pointed to a flashing star in the middle of one of the cemetery's main paths and said, "Please follow me." He walked deeper into the old gravestones, behind the mausoleum.

"How did Crosbie get out, Percy?" Jad asked from the head of their single-file line.

Without turning, Cinn said, "Vice-admiral Crosbie was found by an Inuit hunting party in his tent near Back River. His memoir says he was near death, hallucinating wildly. He imagined himself lying among the white frozen corpses of his crewmates."

"Probably the ghosts of the ones he ate," Jad said.

"The Inuit took him to the trading outpost the crew

had set out to find." Cinn waved his hand with a flourish. "Voila! Survival of the fittest."

"Not how I would've done it," Scott mumbled.

"One never knows what one will do until pushed to one's limits, Mr. Mahoney."

"Yes, Mr. Mahoney," Jad said, looking back at Scott and copying Cinn's tight, drawn speech. "One never knows what one will—*oof!*" He tripped and fell over a low-slung chain surrounding a stainless-steel monolith in the middle of a paved path. Jad rolled from his stomach to his back, his friends asking was he all right, did he hit his head? He twisted his arms to get a look at his elbows. "Man, that kills."

"Your jacket is torn," Sasha said.

Scott stepped over the chain. Jad pulled himself up with Scott's extended hand and brushed crumbs of asphalt and gravel off his knees. He hissed in a breath and saw a small stain of red leach through his jeans.

"You could've warned him," Kinna said to Cinn. He'd moved to the far edge of the monolith, his blue iridescent form shimmering in the reflective surface. While it was narrow enough for a person to wrap her arms around, its top was out of reach. Kinna guessed it was at least four feet taller than Cinn.

"I did try to communicate the hazard, to all of you," he said. "My connection to the Virtokens must have briefly malfunctioned." He turned to Sasha. "I believe you said you were having signal problems yourself, Ms. Balakov?" With barely a breath in between, he continued, "Are you ready to begin your next story?"

"Your company will be getting a strongly-worded text

from me over this," Sasha said, bending to look at Jad's knee while he shooed her away. "You better do the same, Kinna. This was your idea. Look at him, his elbows are bleeding, too."

Kinna frowned and rolled her eyes. "Jad, are you going to be okay? Want to take a break before we go into the next one?"

"Maybe we should stop," Sasha said before Jad could answer.

"Hey."

"Wait a minute."

Kinna and Scott spoke over each other, followed by Jad's, "Definitely not."

"Babe, you're bleeding," Sasha said. "You could've bashed your teeth out."

"But I didn't." He flashed his teeth at her like a wolf. "A few scratches, Sash. Don't worry about it."

"But—"

"Unless you want to leave," Jad said. "Is it getting to you?"

"No."

"Good. Let's do this then. I'm ready."

Kinna thought Sasha had more to say by the firm bite she gave her lip, but settled for glaring at Cinn instead. She anchored herself to Jad with a firm grip on his hand. Kinna had been telling Sasha forever that she fussed too much over Jad. The guy was built like a bear. He didn't need looking after. If he were more like Scott, big in the brain instead of the body, maybe Kinna would get it. Although, she had to admit Scott surprised her tonight. She was shocked when he took her up on her invitation to come here and half expected him to chicken out after the first sim. He was totally holding his own. Kinna looked at him standing next to Jad, his head topping out at the taller guy's shoulder, hands jammed in his jacket. He might be shorter than Jad, but she'd never noticed before that his shoulders were pretty broad. She stepped over the chain and walked to his side.

"Hi," she said.

"Hi?" Scott replied, dragging the word out and looking at her sidelong.

"Nothing," she said. "Just wanted to say hi."

He cut her a glance that clearly meant "all right, weirdo" and asked Cinn to tell them about the monolith.

"Indeed, if you have finished chatting," Cinn said. He looked at each of them, his pointy eyebrows lifted.

"I think he wants an answer," Jad said.

"Yes?" Kinna offered. The others nodded.

"Excellent. The comfort of our guests is paramount. First let me tell you about the symbolism of the monolith in spiritual circles."

As Cinn explained, Scott whispered to Kinna, "Was he being sarcastic? Comfort of guests? After Jad did that faceplant?"

Kinna responded out of the corner of her mouth. "I don't know. Sasha said something earlier, too. Like he was getting an attitude."

Scott nodded. "Yeah, I saw that too. Was there anything about that in the simulation info or reviews?"

Kinna shook her head. "I read a bunch of the comments, but I didn't see anything there. Why, what are you thinking?"

"I don't know. Nothing." He rubbed his Virtoken.

"I am sure Mr. Mahoney and Ms. Chaytor would agree."

Their heads snapped up. Cinn was staring at them.

"Yes?" Scott said.

"Exactly," Cinn replied. "So, what better shape to use for this monument than one designed to both invoke time-lessness and command attention? You may come closer and read the inscription."

Sasha's flashlight found it first, about five feet from the bottom of the monument, engraved into the stainless steel. Kinna read it aloud:

**THIS SCULPTURE
IS DEDICATED TO
ALL MISSING PERSONS.
MAY ALL RELATIVES
AND FRIENDS
WHO VISIT FIND
CONTINUING STRENGTH
AND HOPE.**

"I've never seen a memorial like this before," Kinna said.

"Bit grim isn't it?" Scott said. "Putting it in a grave-yard? You don't know if your missing loved one is alive or dead, but you come to the place where all the bodies are buried to have a think about them?"

Cinn sighed. "I did not place the monument, Mr. Mahoney, nor was the Cramon Cemetery Experience crafted with information on why this memorial was placed here. Shall I continue?"

Scott put his hands in front of him in mock defense. "Sure. Whatever. I was just making a point." Kinna shot him a look and tilted her head at Cinn. It screamed, "See? That's what I was talking about."

"While there are countless missing persons whose stories should be told, the namesake of the foundation that erected this monument disappeared under particularly curious circumstances." Cinn pointed to a section of smaller writing under the main inscription:

COMMISSIONED BY
THE ADRIANA SCALA
MEMORIAL TRUST

"It is her story you will live through tonight."

SECLUSIONS

Hi Mom, hi Dad. It's me. Addy. That's so dumb; like you're not looking right at me! I got this camcorder for my trip and figure this is as good a way as any to test it out before I leave tomorrow. It's, ah, September. The ninth, I think? Two thousand one. Obviously. God this is awkward. How do people work on-camera for a living?

I know I didn't leave on the best terms. I've been thinking about how to make you understand how important my work is; not just to me, but everyone. There's so much you don't know, can't see. When I got to the farmhouse yesterday, I decided I'd read you something, I guess you'd call it an essay. Maybe it's my manifesto! How cool would that be: *The Seclusions Manifesto*. I started writing it when I got to campus last week and added to it in Cragg City last night, after I got back from the hospital. It's my first try at putting together everything I've learned.

Please have an open mind.

Okay. Here we go.

You probably haven't heard of my grandmother,

Adriana Maria Scala, née Drakos. She was famous for fifteen minutes as the only unrecovered body from The Ichor Peaks Incident in November 1951. I say unrecovered body, because everyone naturally assumed she was dead, given the broken bloody mess the search party found at the expedition camp and the gruesome condition of the other bodies. Her sister, Samara, wasn't able to tell them any different; Samara physically survived the happenings in the Peaks long enough to be rescued, but her mind anchored itself in those mountains and never came home.

No less unusual than the circumstances of Adriana's disappearance was the life she led for a woman of her time. She was born January 19, 1917, into a family of wealthy wool merchants. After she married sheep farmer Alex Scala in 1937, a decision her parents questioned but ultimately gave in to, she moved to the tiny community of Keeping in the foothills of the Rocky Mountains. She thrived in the cool, moist air that swept down the highlands. The never-ending fields of tiny yellow and purple flowers carpeting the meadows in spring delighted her. She leaned into the harsh outdoor life. While her husband farmed, Adriana honed hunting and trapping skills. In winter, she would snowshoe into the forest alone, cut firewood, and drag it home on a sled.

When her parents passed away suddenly, Adriana sent for her younger sister, Samara. The woman was just as taken as Adriana with the rugged, demanding foothill lifestyle. Adriana taught her the skills of an outdoorswoman. Samara dressed the way Adriana taught her to dress, moved the way Adriana taught her to move, rode the way Adriana taught her to ride. The two became inseparable companions. It was nothing for Alex to have the house to himself for a week or more while the two women went into the back country to bag elk and rabbits.

If you're thinking a woman with Adriana's physical interests would lack an active inner life, you'd be wrong. She was insatiably curious. She took a room's worth of books with her when she moved to Keeping. My grandfather had to build an extension on their house to shelve them. She'd make special two-day trips to the library in nearby Cragg City (usually with Samara, always on horseback, camping along the way) and the staff got so used to her, they'd give her longer library loans, to account for the distance she had to travel.

She recorded thoughts and events from her day-to-day life in her journals, but most of the space was devoted to her passions: religion, mysticism, and mythology. Her earliest journals were filled with reflections on Christianity. As she became a young woman, her interests broadened to religions she seldom encountered, such as Judaism and Islam, Taoism and Shintoism. After she moved to Keeping, marginalized and scorned spiritualities, like the Dreamtime of Australian Aboriginal people and rituals of Indigenous peoples, increasingly occupied her mind, along with a mix of paganisms and the classical polytheisms of Greeks and Romans. Her journaling style also shifted at this point — she started including sketches of religious symbols, temples, churches, drawing arrows and circles to connect ideas on the pages. Cut-outs of maps and newspaper articles were glued inside.

I discovered all this about Adriana Maria Scala when I found her journals in our basement. Lucky for me, she had a son, Simon, my dad, about six months before she vanished. Lucky for me, he gathered her journals into plastic tubs after my grandfather got Alzheimer's and had to go into a home and Dad cleaned out the old family farmhouse in Keeping.

[And lucky for me, you never sold this house, Dad, because I wouldn't be in it now, recording this video. The place stinks of wood rot and I'm pretty sure an animal crawled under the floorboards to die in the past week. The roof's been leaking into the kitchen and the porch out front has collapsed. Not much of a spot, I know, but I'll be on my way after tonight. Hopefully the truce between me and the raccoons nesting in the chimney will last until then.]

Opening Adriana's journals was like cracking the blinds in a dark room on a blistering sunny morning. A million-watt light shone on my family history. Until I read them, my collected knowledge of my father's family was: Grandpa Alex died of Alzheimer's when I was five years old; I was named after my grandmother; she wore pants instead of dresses; she disappeared on a skiing trip; and her sister Samara had survived that trip, but died shortly after. Oh! I also knew what they'd all looked like: there was a black and white picture of my grandmother, Grandpa and Samara on our mantle. They were standing on the porch of this farmhouse, Grandpa smiling wide, a lady on each arm. To see them, you'd know the women were related – same bright hair, same high wide-set cheekbones, same average height and stocky build - but a careful look suggested they weren't alike in temper: Adriana's eyes bored into the lens, while Samara's were soft and looked beyond the camera. My grandmother's free arm was elbow out, hand on her hip; Samara's hands were folded at her waist. It was the only picture of them my dad had.

He wasn't big on his family's history. I guess being an only child, with his mom long gone and his dad locked inside his own mind for so many years, Dad figured there wasn't much for him to talk about.

He was *so* wrong.

My grandmother's journals triggered wildfire in the dry tinder of my eleven-year-old imagination. I didn't understand it all at that age. The ideas she played with were too big. My synapses weren't up to processing them. But I couldn't get enough of her stories about life on the land — learning to trap from a wrinkled-up moonshine maker, being stalked by cougars on hunting trips — and the drawings and maps, no matter what they were about, kept me hurrying to bed each night to trace them with my fingers.

My parents encouraged me at first. My dad thought it was a good way to get to know my grandmother, like he had known her through his father's stories, and learn about her life in Keeping. I had so many questions. How many guns did she have? What's a pika and does it taste like chicken? She didn't really cut off her toe, did she? What did she do on weekends if there was no TV? My dad laughed at most of them, but always answered.

I heard him talking about it to my mom one night after I'd gone to bed.

"It's like she's found a new best friend," my dad said.

"Are you sure about letting her read them all, Simon?" Mom asked. "She hasn't touched another book in months.

You know how she gets fixated on things."

My father snorted. "Yeah. Something else she shares with my mother. Goes with the name, I guess."

"Next thing she'll be out trapping squirrels in the backyard and asking me how to cook them."

"I'll skip dinner that night," my father said, chuckling. They were quiet for a minute. When he spoke again, he wasn't laughing. "Addy won't understand half of it, Evie. I'll keep an eye on her. I…" he cleared his throat. "You know how complicated it is. But it's been nice to talk to someone about her. Mom."

Dad was right. At first, half of the writing did go over my head or bored me. I turned a corner when I was fourteen. Mom's sister got diagnosed with cancer that year. Aunt Shelly was sick for a long time. She lost all her hair and couldn't keep food down. Mom was crying about it. When I picked through Adriana's journals, I started to pay more attention to the entries about her own sister, Samara. The ones written while they were preparing for their expedition to Ichor Peaks especially.

Journal Excerpt, Adriana Scala
October 22, 1951

"*We leave for the expedition in less than a week. I've heard from our guide, Mr. Templeton. He assures me that the extreme weather will not delay our departure, that the excess snowfall will assist our progress, so long as a warm spell does not descend. The three other expeditioners will meet us in Torsville, where we will pick up the trail. As the day approaches, I grow more fearful for Samara. The dream…I am having it every night now. A cloud of black, thick as a billow of soot, just as insubstan-*

*tial. It descends from a thicket of wood in the Pass. It does not
mark the snow, but has all the appearance of crawling toward
us, like a wolf spider hunting insects. Perhaps it is a spider in
its own realm; the closer it is, the more distinctly I see the tiny
round marks suspended within it, thousands of them, shimmering and rolling like marbles in a socket. It comes. I cannot stop
it. It comes until it takes us."*

Journal Excerpt, Adriana Scala
October 24, 1951
*"For myself, this trip is a necessity; I must know, even if it
means I do not return to my husband and son. For Samara, it
is merely an adventure to share with me. I have warned her of
the risks, showed her my research, expressed my concerns. For
all that, she is a grown woman and will make her own decision.
If she comes to harm, or the worst happens and she does not
survive, I hope I am taken with her, as I do not know how I will
live without her."*

Like my dad, I'm an only child. I've never had a sib-
ling to tease or fight with or worry about. My mother's
state over her sister and my grandmother's torment over
Samara swirled into one big tornado of emotion and confusion. One evening I stood in front of my father demanding to know how Samara had died and what was so important my grandmother had to drag her sister out into
the wilderness. He took his glasses off and laid them on
the kitchen table on top of the crossword puzzle he'd been
doing. He repeated the story he'd told me before, that
both my great-aunt and grandmother had gone on a skiing tour, an avalanche hit their camp a couple of nights

into the trip, my grandmother was never found, Samara died from her injuries after she got back to the farm.

"But why were they even up there? Your mother had a baby at home. Why was it so important?"

Dad tried to explain postpartum depression to me. As a kid it was hard to understand how having a baby could make a mother – and sometimes a father – depressed, restless and anxious. How it could be so bad in some people they didn't sleep, got paranoid, had delusions. I told him it didn't make sense, not for Adriana. I kept pressing. He circled back to the same answers and I felt their half-truths in my bones. Our conversation was on the cusp of becoming an argument when I realized my grandmother's journals, the parts that had bored me up to then, probably held the answers. Full books I'd flipped through but never read were sitting under my bed at that very moment.

"Fine!" I said to him. "I'll go find out for myself." It was a brilliant line to stomp away on, but I was dumb not to see what he'd do after I said it. He pushed back from the table so fast, his chair tipped over. After he scrambled in the pantry for a second, he blew past me and took the steps two at a time to get to my bedroom.

"I'm burning these," my father shouted as he hauled armfuls of the journals out from under my bed and tossed them into a black garbage bag. "Her lunatic fantasies will ruin you just like they ruined her!"

He didn't torch them. He stored them in a locked filing cabinet and forbid me to think about them until I was old enough to draw a pension.

Being a kid is mostly crap: told when to eat, when to sleep, where you can go. An eighteen-year prison sentence. But! One great thing: everyone underestimates you. Mom and Dad could never have dreamed I'd figure out how to pick the lock on the filing cabinet. You really can do it with a paperclip, just like in the movies.

Any time my parents left me home alone, I snuck a journal out of the cabinet and sat on the ratty sofa in the basement, taking notes, with our Doberman, Rex, curled next to me. Rex had the adorable ability to sense when my parents' car turned up our street and he'd bound up the stairs to wait for them at the window. I always had plenty of time to put the book back, lock the cabinet, and set-up in front of the living room TV before they came in the door.

[Mom and Dad, I can admit to myself now that, even though I was interested in what Grandma had to write, I started off sneaking the journals mostly because I was giving you a tiny poke with an imaginary finger every time I turned a page. Here in Keeping, with the supplies I'll need laid out on the floor of the extension Grandpa built for Grandma's books - the only dry floor in this place – I can see it was also a way for me to feel closer to her, and even to you, Dad. I'm sorry we couldn't find a way to talk about it back then.]

It's hard to imagine a time when I wasn't completely obsessed by Adriana's life work. She'd developed a theory, you see, that sunk its claws into my grey matter.

Three years of high school passed in a blur. I spent my nights and weekends holed up in libraries and my bedroom and the basement, writing, reading, writing, reading. You'd think my grades would've suffered, but it was the opposite: every subject offered insight to help me understand my grandmother's work and disappearance. Science connected me to Earth's natural forces and systems she wrote about. Cultural studies shed light on the religion, history and philosophy my grandmother wrapped herself in. I admit I almost flunked Phys Ed, but even that would've come in handy for what I've got ahead of me. I wish I'd put more effort into it.

But I only had so much time. Something had to give.

I lost my junior high friends when I stopped going out with them. I didn't have time to make more in my last three years of school. Parents are always on their kids' backs to stay out of trouble, watch less TV, play fewer video games. Lies, lies, lies. They don't really want that. If mine had, they would've left it at gently nudging me to hang out with friends or take a night off reading and watch a couple of movies. Instead, they levelled up, forcing weekend sleepovers with my cousins on me and giving pointed gifts, like a PlayStation and gift certificates to the bowling alley. When they found out I wasn't planning to attend my prom, they sent me to a behaviour specialist for a bunch of tests. When news came back I was well adjusted and big brained, my parents changed gears faster than a race car driver. Suddenly I was an eccentric genius. This suited me fine, as they put all their efforts into picking out a university worthy of me and left me alone.

[Sorry, Mom and Dad, but I have to tell it how it happened.]

So, what the hell was so interesting about my grandmother's work that it sucked me in like quicksand?

Adriana's research led her to believe that even though there have been thousands of religions throughout history, all of them originated with a small number of beings in specific corners of the world: gods, deities, spirits, immortals; whatever you want to call them. In the beginning, they lived and travelled among humans. Each culture encountering them in person or through stories put its own spin on who these beings were, what they looked like, how they acted. Presto! Thousands of religions.

Long before walking, talking humans appeared, these beings evolved to feed off the natural systems on our planet: solar radiation, magnetic fields, kinetic energy of the Earth's rotation. They were perfectly adapted. But once humanoids developed, a new energy became available: mental energy. Petition, prayer; the devotion showed to these beings acted on them like a drug. Over time, they became less efficient at living off natural systems and more reliant on worship. As humans evolved and civilizations grew, the beings relinquished more of their physical space; they'd grown lazy and addicted to the adulation. If the prayers kept coming, they saw no reason to fight the intrusion.

But they took notice of the rise of reason and science. For the first time, they felt weak. They played with "dreadful visitations", trying to put humans back in their place – an exploding Krakatoa here, a Spanish Flu pandemic there. Humans took no notice. In fact, they continued to become more spiritually independent and spread further across the globe. When the beings tried to wean themselves off worship, they found they couldn't summon more than the basest power. They had poisoned themselves on prayer for so long, they could only eke out a marginal existence off the world's natural systems. Their last stand came in the twentieth century. Hoping to drive humanity back to their gods through horror and terror, they stoked two world wars. During and after this failure to start a new dark age, my grandmother theorized the beings conceded and each retreated to remote parts of the world, surviving off the meagre amounts of worship left to them and what little lifeforce they could draw from nature.

All of this sucked me in the same way books like *American Gods*, *Journey to the Center of the Earth*, and *The Odyssey* grabbed me and pulled me into fantastical land- and mindscapes.

But here's where it got really interesting: my grand-mother had mashed this theory together with patterns of human migration and growth of civilizations through the ages. Then she layered on research into areas of the world with weirdly high incidents of death, disappearance, and mechanical failures, or where seemingly natural phenom-ena kept people away (whether they were age-old areas hostile to humans or appeared suddenly after the war).

The types of places said to be cursed.

She made notes on the Corryvreckan Maelstrom off the coast of Scotland, a whirlpool that sucks anything near it straight to the bottom of the ocean. She sketched and made notes on the Tsingy De Bemaraha in Madagascar. I can still see her scrawled note on the margin of a maga-zine article about these forests of giant limestone needles: "Tsingy = where one cannot walk barefoot". In her day, it was hardly visited by locals or foreigners; the razor-sharp rocks shredded climbing gear and even a small stumble could see you impaled on a jagged stone. In a remote cor-ner of Mongolia, there's Tam (roughly translates to "hell" in English): a giant crater of fire that began burning in the mid-1940s. The government's story was the crater was part of an enormous gas field that caught fire from a lightning strike and continued to burn off methane gas. My grandmother called poppycock on that. She had sketched out a part of the Atlantic Ocean that covered the waters between Florida, Puerto Rico and Bermuda and flagged it as an area where an unusual number of ships and aircraft disappeared - my grandmother was onto the Bermuda Triangle a decade ahead of everyone else.

Grandma Adriana believed these sites were the last bastions of once-great beings. Pieces of the material world they refused to give over to human beings. Places where they drew what little power they could from land, water, air and fire to keep people away or punish those who came. She called the sites "Seclusions".

Out of the two dozen she found, the one she dug into the most was Ichor Peaks, a small group of mountains around the Drake Pass in the Rocky Mountains.

There's no Everest or Kilimanjaro in this cluster, no crazy rock shapes that show up in travel brochures. The only remarkable thing about this area is the weirdly high number of people who either die or disappear there. Not only hikers and skiers, but also pilots whose helicopters crash while searching for the missing, police and rangers who go in to remove human remains. Even the searches themselves go oddly wrong: bodies turning up in areas already searched, sniffer dogs unable to trace scents. My grandmother found more than fifty events there over a seven-year period.

The map she put in her journal marked each event

with a red dot. They merge into one giant bloody blob over Ichor Peaks.

I read every page she'd written, each note, flipping between books, trying to fill in the gaps in Adriana's story. Why had she fixated on the Ichor Peaks Seclusion? Why the urgency of her trip, when summer made for easier travel and she had a newborn at home? I never bought Dad's postpartum depression explanation. And the biggest question of all: what happened to her and Samara in the Peaks?

It's not clear from her journals, but I think she focused on Ichor Peaks because she felt close to it. Not just physically – it was only 200 kilometres away as the crow flies – but spiritually. From the minute she moved to Keeping, the Rockies were a jagged constant on her horizon. The journals mentioned over and over again how she was *in thrall* of the foothills and forests in the mountains' shadow. You know the definition of "in thrall"? To be controlled or deeply influenced by a person or object. Passages she wrote show her infatuation.

Journal Excerpt, Adriana Scala
July 11, 1948
"A part of me has become the land. The earth collects in my blood as readily as in the creases of my palm."

Journal Excerpt, Adriana Scala
October 2, 1942
"To hunt is not so much to see animal tracks, but feel them on my skin; the heat, pressure and shape of them tell me what I am hunting, when it passed and which direction it will go."

The woman was deep.

Her choice of timing was harder to understand. It wasn't until I did a timeline of the unusual events my grandmother had pulled together that I saw a pattern she must have seen: the incidents were happening less frequently over time. From 1948 to 1950, there were only a couple of reported missing persons per year. One near-miss between two airplanes. In 1951, up until she left for her November trip to the Peaks, there were none.

My grandmother's desk used to be in front of a window that overlooked the Rockies. She described the way the gunmetal clouds hung over the jagged teeth of the mountains in the distance. Who could look at that view every day and not understand, in her soul, it was the perfect place to disappear if you wanted to hide from humanity? I've imagined her sitting there, at her desk, chewing on the mystery of Ichor Peaks' declining incident numbers. She must've reached the same conclusion I did: the power of whatever being was in the Seclusion was fading. Maybe the being had become mortal and was dying.

Ichor Peaks was close, but the window to explore it and its secrets was closing. Adriana made her plans.

[Just like I'm finalizing mine, tonight. I wish I could've seen this place like you did when you were young, Dad. Her desk is gone, obviously, but I'm standing right where it used to be, in the extension Grandpa built for her books. Her books! I can't tell you how many times I've wished you hadn't donated those. If I'd had them at my fingertips it would've cut my research time in half.]

Her journals couldn't tell me what happened in the

Peaks, of course. They ended the day before she and Samara left to travel to Torsville with this entry:

Journal Excerpt, Adriana Scala
October 27, 1951

"Samara and I had a fierce fight. With our departure tomorrow looming, I was sick with worry for her. I could not eat this whole day. Months ago, when I conceived of this trip, I was concerned this day would arrive and I would be so anguished at the thought of leaving Simon and Alex that I would forgo the whole trip. But it is Samara — Samara, who is to bear all the risks with me — that has galvanized my fear. The creature will not leave my dreams. It has developed an unnatural taste for her when it descends on us in the Pass. I begged her to reconsider. When she refused, I told her I could not look after both myself and her on the journey. Unfortunately, she knows her quality as an outdoorswoman and she laughed in my face. Finally, I told her I would not go. She stared at me. And I tried, so very hard, not to show how crushing it was to say those words. To deny myself this trip was akin to admitting I had been wasting years of my life on frivolity. But I meant it. To keep her safe, I would do anything. She stared for what felt like minutes, then she told me she was leaving in the morning for Ichor Peaks, with or without me. And so now I am trapped in a net of my own making. Petitioning a god defies everything I have learned over the course of my research. But I do not know what else to do. Whichever of you inhabits this Seclusion, I pray you will allow my sister to return home safely."

[Reading it out loud to you guys, knowing what I know after visiting the hospital in Cragg City, I'm covered in goosebumps. Look! All the way up my arm. The

city is big enough to have a mall and a bunch of stores that sold the supplies and maps I needed. This camera was on sale, but I still had to put it on the credit card you gave me for emergencies when I left for university. Sorry. I hope you don't get wind of it for a few days. It's getting near nine o'clock. I've got to get to bed soon if I want to make an early start in the morning. There's so much more to tell.]

Without Adriana's journals to guide me, I spent hours at the library, flipping between microfiche, magazines, and books to learn about The Ichor Peaks Incident itself. I inhaled anything I could get my hands on.

As much material as there was to read, the facts were bare. Six people, including my grandmother, her sister, and the guide, Joseph Templeton, left on November 1, 1951, for a fourteen-day skiing trip into Ichor Peaks. All were experienced cross-country skiers; all were outfitted with the best outdoor winter gear. The single tent the group would sleep in (unusual for the time with both men and women on the trek, but necessary for keeping warm at night) was secured to a sled Templeton would tow. My grandmother and her sister had bought identical skis, snowshoes, and down jackets for the trip and Samara packed two fresh loaves of cornbread for the ride from Keeping to Torsville, where they would meet the others. The villagers saw the expeditioners in a pub the night before their departure clinking their glasses loudly, sending up cries of "Cheers!" and "To luck!". They remarked one woman at the table tended more toward quietly sipping her drink and kept her intense dark eyes focused on the pub's fireplace for most of the evening.

When the expedition didn't return by its scheduled date of November 15, the local rescue team started to assemble. They waited a day before starting a search, to account for short delays the missing group might have encountered. The weather had been fine – chilly and clear – so there was no concern a storm had caused the expedition any trouble and it was known they'd packed more than the required fourteen days' worth of food. The search party entered the mountains on November 16. On November 18, they entered Drake Pass, the only way through Ichor Peaks.

They found the first body mid-morning.

A young searcher named Michael Leffrett saw the peak of a green canvas tent behind a snowdrift. When he approached, his ski tangled in something in the snow and he fell, his nose almost pressing to the blue-sheened, frozen face of Joseph Templeton, the expedition guide. The corpse's eyes and mouth were wide open, his body bent so his feet almost touched the back of his head, making clear his spine was snapped. He was wearing long-johns and one sock.

Two other bodies were found near the tent. Both were dressed only in underwear and none wore boots. Aillis Boyen's neck was cracked and her jaw ripped almost off her face. Her husband, Pat, had both his arms broken up behind his back, like someone put him in a double arm hold and pushed too far. Both shoulders were dislocated.

There was no sign of Georgina duYari, Samara, or my grandmother on the open slopes of the pass. A set of staggering footprints was followed into the tree line a kilometre from the camp. The search party found a fir tree with the branches removed up to a height of four or five feet.

Signs of soot were found at its base, but the remains of the
fire itself were never located. It wasn't clear whether the
branches were ripped off to use in the fire, or if someone
had tried to climb the tree to either get a better viewpoint,
or escape something. Deeper in the woods, the ground
fell away sharply into a ravine. The snow hadn't built up
down there yet. Rescuers had to repel down and negoti-
ate on foot the unfrozen river still running at its bottom.
DuYari was found on the riverbank, naked except for her
socks. Her winter gear and underclothes were spread
around her in a spiral pattern. Her eye sockets were empty bloody pits. Her tongue was missing.

They almost missed Samara on their first sweep
through the ravine. If one of the searchers hadn't stopped
to take a leak next to a wide, flat slab of rock at the base
of the ravine wall, if he hadn't happened to look at the
thick overhang of roots and grass built up over it, if he
hadn't bent in curiosity to find the small cave created by
the meeting of the rock and the overhang, he never would
have seen the motionless lump that was Samara wrapped
in her coat.

This searcher became a semi-famous alpine adventur-
er years later; well-known enough to have his autobiogra-
phy published. In it, he describes finding Samara Drakos
in the ravine.

Excerpt from Alone in the Mountains *by Robert Grandy*
p. 153-155
*"At first, I thought I was looking at a boulder, rounded off
like so many others by the river's action. I shone my flashlight
into the cave and, when I saw the thing was black, jumped back*

two feet, thinking I'd stumbled onto a black bear's den. By the time my heart dropped out of my throat and sank back behind my ribs, I'd realized what I was seeing was fabric, not fur. I crab-walked forward, thinking of that poor woman lying on the river-bank and the mangled bodies we'd found at the camp, preparing myself for what I was likely to find. I grabbed the edge of the cloth - a coat, as it turned out – and pulled it slowly toward me. A blue-tinged shoulder was revealed, an arm, torso. The body wore undergarments, but they were torn and shredded. I could trace most of the bones under the skin of her emaciated body. She (who could it be other than either Samara or Adriana Scala) didn't move as I pulled the jacket all the way down to reveal her legs, covered in long-johns, and her delicate bare feet. Their soles were bloody and raw and the big toe on her right foot was missing.

Her name was embroidered on the inside collar of the coat. "Samara," I whispered. "We're here to save you." I said it again, louder, when she didn't respond. Taking her thigh gently, I shook her. Nothing. Thinking she was dead, I stood up to shout to the rest of the party that I'd found another body.

When her hand wrapped around my ankle, the shock was like touching a live wire.

I've faced grizzlies. I've watched my rope fray while hang-ing on a cliff face. I swear to you, no danger in all my life had me shrieking the way I did when she grabbed me. I had a split second to take in her mutilated hand, the stump of her ring fin-ger and pinky hanging on by a thin strip of skin, before I fell to the ground and convulsed.

I came back to myself lying on my side, one of the crew kneel-ing beside me. I hadn't passed out. More like went to another place for a minute. Not unlike the lady the rest of the rescuers were trying to ease out of the cave. Her high, wailing screams started the moment they tried to move her. As each part of her emerged, a new injury was revealed: a broken ankle, a lacerated thigh (fortunately not deep enough to hit the artery and stuffed with an assortment of moss and leaves), broken ribs under a riot of red and purple skin. But her face. It's hard to write about, even after all these years. On the right side, her skin was in ribbons from her forehead to her chin. The blood had long since dried into dark crusty furrows. I couldn't tell if the eye was still in its socket. A middle-aged, muscled-out man in our party fainted dead away when he caught full sight of her.

When she was finally free of the cave and cocooned in rescue blankets, she went silent. They secured her to the wooden rescue board in preparation for pulling her up the side of the ravine. I was tucking the blankets around her before they hoisted her. Her good eye rolled my way. There was intent lucidity in it. "Don't leave her," she said. The eye rolled back toward the sky, unfocused. I understand she never spoke another word."

It was almost nightfall by the time the rescuers finished in the ravine. In the morning, the team would split into two: one group staying to continue searching for Adriana, the other taking Samara back to Torsville. I've imagined the rescue team setting up camp in the pass that night, surrounded by tarped bodies laid out in the snow, a catatonic woman nearby who was likely to die among them that night, if not on the two-day trip back to civilization. I see them sitting around a fire, cooking food they don't eat, trying to explain what they'd found. An avalanche seemed to be the only thing they could all agree on, but there were no signs an avalanche had happened any time in the last several weeks. And why were the bodies almost naked? The expedition camp was littered with the coats, heavy pants, hats, boots, and other gear brought in by the six skiers. Why would they take it off? Why was the expedition tent cut open *from the inside*?

That first night in the pass was probably the starting point for the odder theories people would come up with over the years to explain the fate of The Ichor Peaks Expedition. Aliens. Sasquatch. Science experiment gone wrong. Secret military operation. Weird as those sounded to the average person, they were tame next to the explanation I had, based on my grandmother's writings and research: the expedition was attacked by a pissed off immortal creature who rose from its den of seclusion. It swept through the camp, consigning all the trespassers, except Samara, to one or several fates: twisting their bodies until they snapped, tearing and peeling their flesh, scaring them far enough from the camp, so fast, they couldn't grab their gear, driving them so far away, they couldn't find their way back and succumbed to hypothermia. My grandmother, although technically recorded as missing, was also obviously killed in one or a combination of those ways.

Being only a theory, it wasn't fully satisfying, but it was destined to be the only answer I'd have. At least, it was until I found the video tape.

On my last day home before leaving for university, I went to the basement and opened the filing cabinet to box up my grandmother's journals, hoping my father wouldn't notice they were gone until after I'd left. My parents were out, so I wasn't being quiet or careful. A heavy box had been put in front of the cabinet, blocking a small part of the lower drawer. I shoved it a bit, got lazy and tried to force the drawer open past it. It worked. Too well. The drawer resisted, then pulled free of the box, past the stops on the cabinet, and slid onto the concrete floor. I blinked, stared at it like I expected it to perform another trick, then glanced at the open space in the cabinet where it used to be. Sitting on the smooth metal bottom, dropped from a drawer who knew how many years ago, was a VHS tape. Written in bold black marker on its white label was, "Investigation Nation: March 13, 1985. Ichor." I had a vague memory of the show coming on at night around my bedtime when I was a kid, but my parents told me the unsolved crimes and freaky events the show talked about were too scary for me to watch.

I sat on the living room couch, the tape humming in the VHS player and the TV spitting static until a commercial of Brooke Shields hawking Arrid Extra Dry squiggled onto the screen. The picture cleared as the tinkling theme music for Investigation Nation started and the sunk-eyed, bald host delivered his intro, walking through the mist in a trench coat: "*November, 1951. Six skiers set off for a trip in the Rocky Mountains. When they failed to return, a search was called. What rescuers found continues to confound scientists and haunt the people touched by the events. Join me as we investigate what really happened during The Ichor Peaks Incident.*"

I had no idea this episode existed. No surprise my parents never talked about it. We'd reached a truce over Grandma: I didn't ask, they ignored my interest in her and her work, so long as I stayed on track to go to Amsteldon University in the fall. I watched the episode with the

satisfaction of a dog snatching a pork chop off the kitch-
en counter, but only gave it partial attention; the show
wouldn't tell me anything I didn't already know. I'd lived
this topic for years, knew every angle. After about twenty
minutes, the host was wrapping it up. I squat in front of
the TV, getting ready to pop the tape out and put it back
where I found it.

*"But what of Samara Drakos, the sole survivor, and Adri-
ana Scala, her missing sister? Adriana's son, Simon, refused to
be interviewed for this piece."*

I bet he did, I thought.

My finger was on the eject button when the host blew
my world open like sunbaked roadkill: *"Our attempts to
visit Samara at the William Street Hospital in Cragg City were
rebuffed by hospital administrators."*

What. The. Actual. Flying. Hell.

I shot the tape out of the player and read the label
again. March 1985. Samara hadn't died when she got back
from Ichor Peaks. She was still alive fifteen years ago.

There was nowhere to put my rage in that moment,
so I tried to burn off some energy by finishing packing for
my drive to campus the next day. My hands were shaking
as I put Adriana's journals and the VHS tape into a box.
I put it on top of my suitcases and the boxes of books I'd
stacked in the backseat of my old Honda. I sat on the doorstep of our house in the low evening light and waited. The
fight my dad and I had when he got home was atomic.

**[Dad, I said so many things to you I wish I hadn't
that night. I wish I'd picked up the phone all the times
you've called me since. I was still so angry. I'm not
anymore. Even after going to the hospital and seeing**

Samara, or maybe because of it, I understand why you
kept things from me. But I still wish you'd seen that this
– not just the journey I'll start tomorrow, but the one I've
been on since I found Grandma's journals years ago – is
something we could've done together!

Sorry. I told myself I wouldn't cry when I did this.
Just...give me a sec. I'm so tired. I hope I can sleep to-
night. God, it's late. Let me read you the last of it, then
I have to go.]

I left for university the next day, but my mind was on
a trip to Cragg City. My plan was to unpack my things at
the dorm and leave for the city within a couple of days. I
was still so angry at my father and my thoughts were so
tangled, I thought it would help clear my head if I wrote
all of this down first. In the end I stayed on campus for
a week. I hardly slept those few days, between the time
I spent writing and the dreams I had of snow and blood
and dark, swirling shadows when I tried to rest. When I
was ready to leave, I decided I'd crash the hospital. No
phone calls, no notice. I figured one of two things would
happen: I'd find Samara still alive (I wasn't sure of her age,
but knew she was younger than my grandmother, so likely in her late seventies or early eighties) and be welcomed
by the staff as a great-niece who'd come so far to visit, or
I'd learn Samara had passed away and I could pump them
for information.

Finding out my great-aunt was alive and mostly well
when I arrived at William Street Hospital didn't bring
the simple happiness I expected. When the receptionist
told me Samara's room number and I followed her directions to the north wing of the building, I was wringing

my hands. I thought only old women did that in Victorian novels. But there I was, nerves making me grind my knuckles together and my stomach flip. Some people plan once-in-a-lifetime trips around seeing a holy relic or visiting the famous landmarks of the world. Meeting Samara was my Buddha's Tooth, my Great Wall of China. She was a tangible connection to my grandmother and a living witness to events that had consumed my life for years. How could I have been naïve enough to think meeting her would be anything less than overwhelming?

[I half expected when I showed up at William Street Hospital they'd tell me Samara wasn't allowed to have visitors. I guess you'd hidden her from me for so long, I imagined her as a prisoner locked in a dark cell. Her room is actually beautiful. Bright. You can see the Rockies out her window. But you'd know that, Dad. The staff told me you visit her at least once a year. I'm glad.]

Apparently, my father is quite charming, because dropping his name to Nurse Little on Samara's unit earned me a broad smile and an invitation to ask as many questions as I liked. I found out when Samara arrived at William Street, they put her in a room facing the gardens. She had fits every day. One of the orderlies noticed she would stare at the mountains when she went outside and never make a peep. When they switched her to the room she has now, the fits stopped. I learned Samara had hardly spoken a word in the fifty years she'd been there, but drew prolifically until her hands became too arthritic to hold the dark charcoal and graphite sticks she preferred for her moody abstract artwork.

My heart pounded when the nurse opened the panelled wood door to her room and stood aside to let me in. Samara was sitting in a floral Queen Anne chair facing the window, at an angle to the door.

"Miss Drakos, I've got a surprise for you today," Nurse Little said. "Adriana is here to see you. Simon's daughter." I could swear her shoulders tensed when the nurse said my name, but she was utterly still afterward, so I might have imagined it.

"Addy," I corrected her.

"Addy. Come see me at the desk if you need anything." She left the door open when she stepped out.

Samara didn't turn around or move at all. I walked slowly into the room and slid a straight-backed chair in front of the window next to her so we were both looking outside. Not close enough we would rub elbows - I didn't want to freak her out – but near enough I could look at her out of the corner of my eye.

She wasn't like I expected. All I had to go on were the old picture on the mantle and descriptions of her as the damaged woman they carried out of Drake Pass. Her blond hair was white now, cut short. And her shoulders were tiny and hunched. I noticed her ankle was bent at an unnatural angle. The break hadn't healed properly. No doubt the walker next to her chair was a necessity. Her face was what surprised me most. In my mind, her wound was still bloody and mangled, not pale and polished. The long scars were almost the same colour as her papery white skin. So smooth, like a pearl. Someone must've done a wonder job on her stitches and wound care. I was so happy to see she hadn't lost her eye. I even found out something that hadn't turned up in my research: she'd lost an ear.

"I'm Addy." Stupid. The nurse already introduced me. I tried, "How are you, Aunt Samara?" I didn't think about calling her that, it just came out, and it felt right. She didn't answer, of course. Without a plan for what I was going to say when I saw her, I let the silence stretch out until it got punishing. Then I started talking about myself. My family. I talked about Grandma. The journals. She may as well have been a stone for all the reaction she showed. Her eyes stayed fixed out the window.

I'd been talking for a good hour before I got to telling her about my research into The Ichor Peaks Incident. If I hadn't been shamelessly gawking at the pinkish nubs where her ring and pinky fingers used to be, I would've missed the subtle tensing of her hand on the hard wooden knobs of the armrests. My mouth shut like a trap and my eyes flew to her face. No change. But everything had changed. I could feel it as surely as I can feel the wind shift direction. I sat back in my chair and stared at the windowsill.

"They left her there."

I jumped. Whole body. If anyone had walked in on us then, they would've seen me crowded onto the far side of my chair, a leg curled up as defending myself against the frail, frozen woman next to me.

"I left her there."

The woman was a statue. I was watching her mouth the second time she spoke and damned if I could see her lips move.

I leaned toward her. "It's okay, Aunt Samara. She wouldn't want you feeling bad about...that." What else could I say? Everything in me was avoiding saying the words "dead" and "body". I tentatively laid my hand on hers. When she didn't pull it away, I rubbed it, hoping the contact would comfort her.

"That thing wouldn't let her go."

Boom! Stars flickered in front of my eyes. I went still. If she meant what I thought she meant...

"You mean the spirit, Aunt Samara? The immortal?"

She shuddered. "She prays. For me." She turned her head my way. She still looked beautiful to me, more like the woman in the picture than the mutilated woman from the Peaks. Her eyes bored into mine.

Bits of information cascaded through my mind. Big bits, small bits, tumbling together, ricocheting apart. Years of research layered over one another, folding; edges of mental origami paper coming together to form a single, recognizable thought-shape. The god-creature. It thrived on prayer. Before she left on the expedition, Adriana petitioned it to spare Samara. Maybe she had given it the burst of power it needed to decimate the camp? Even if that wasn't true, she'd have thought it was – everything in her research would point to it. The guilt she must have felt as she watched the sentient cloud of malice snap the members of her party as if they were no more than handfuls of matchsticks.

And then Samara. Her sweet sister who had come on the expedition for her, to satisfy Adriana's obsession. The creature started to savage her. I can hear the words Adriana must've spoken as clearly as if I was standing in Ichor Peaks that night in 1951: "Please, I pray of you, do not kill my sister." Her voice would've been high with panic, but strong. The words that likely set the stage for their pact: "I'll do anything." The only thing a creature like that could want from her was a lifetime – maybe an immortality – of prayer.

She prays. For me.

Samara's life in exchange for Adriana's devotions.

The charge to my body, my brain, from each realization had me out of the chair, marching from one side of the room to the other. Samara shifted in her chair. Small, micro-movements, but clear signs of agitation for a woman who'd hardly stirred since I arrived. The idea of my grandmother still being alive in Ichor Peaks was laughable. To everyone. Except Samara. And me.

I came up next to Samara and laid my hand on her shoulder. She turned her head back to the window, but what little muscle she had was still tense under my fingers. We both looked out at the mountains. I wondered if we were both seeing Adriana with that creature, caught in an endless cycle of supplication. Wondered if this was what Samara imagined every minute she sat looking out this window. I squeezed her shoulder.

"It'll be all right." Saying it unleashed something in me. Empathy. Gratitude. Affection. I was only able to find some of the words to describe it later, when I put pen to paper in my hotel room. In the moment, it was simply an enormous rush of emotion that filled my chest and made my head spin. Through the act of writing this, I came to understand what it was: my entire being filling with pure, uncomplicated purpose.

I bent and kissed Samara on her ruined cheek. She moved and I felt upward pressure under my hand where it still rested on her shoulder, like she was trying to stand. She looked up at me again, frowning. I smiled and turned to leave. Before I got to the door, a low keening sound came from behind me. I glanced back at Samara. She was reaching for her walker, struggling to pull herself up out of the chair. When I kept going, the sound evolved into a jarring, strident shriek. Nurse Little hurried past me in the doorway, cooing soothing sounds to Samara. I could barely hear them over what had become full-throated screaming. It seemed impossible her tiny body could make such a sound.

That's all of it, folks. The whole manuscript so far. I ran out of writing steam last night and between shopping for supplies this morning and having to drive up here, I haven't had a chance to get back at it. I'll have a lot more to add to it when I get back from Ichor Peaks.

I didn't mean for it to upset Samara. I didn't even tell her I was going after Grandma; she just felt it, I guess. I hope she was able to settle down after I left.

How is it past eleven o'clock?

And…yep, the battery is getting low on this thing.

I have to be stingy with the batteries I've got, I don't want to run out while I'm in the Peaks. But I had to do this video for you guys, so you'd understand why I have to do this. It's helped me, too. Laying the whole story out in one go really reinforces how much sense it makes. How right it is.

Dad, I know you have all these tangly feelings about Grandma. Maybe it would've helped you to help me all these years? Maybe you would've changed your mind about your mom being a, what did you call her? Narcissistic lunatic? The funny thing is, you're partly right about her work: Grandma's ideas *are* dangerous. But not because they're crazy; they're dangerous because they're real and *nobody takes them seriously*. You read the news, you see it all over TV: the world is falling apart. People are lost and lonely and the ones who use religion to get through it are becoming more fanatical. What do you think is happening to those beasts hiding in the Seclusions? They're getting stronger the more fundamentalist their petitioners become. Most of the Seclusions Grandma found have gotten more active in the last ten years than they were the forty years before that. Even Ichor Peaks. Look it up yourself. Yes, I know that makes my trip there more dangerous, but I also know more than anyone else what to expect there, what's waiting. More even than Grandma did.

Don't worry, I'm not dumb enough to go climbing up there alone. I'm joining an expedition with five other people. We'll check in with the local search and rescue when we leave. Shouldn't be more than ten days; five in, five out. I'm going to ask them to give you a call the day after we set out, in case you call my dorm looking for me. You'll freak out when you find out where I've gone, but at least you'll know where I am.

I don't know when you'll get this tape. I'm dropping it in the mail when I get to Torsville tomorrow. I'll talk to you when I get back. Love you both.

5

Screaming greeted Kinna as her awareness returned to the graveyard.

"Sasha! What? What is it?" Jad's voice, frantic.

Kinna spun in a circle, unbalanced, colliding with Scott. His arms wrapped around her. They stumbled together until they came up against the monument. The screaming stopped. The sensory vacuum it left focused Kinna's senses on the feel of Scott's chest pressed into hers, the mild soapy-citrus scent on the skin of his neck. That Scott, her friend since they were eight years old, had a *feel* and a *scent* was so odd, her lips parted in surprise. Scott's eyes met hers, dropped to her mouth.

"I saw it. I swear to God I saw it."

Sasha's breathy voice unravelled the tension tying Kinna's attention to Scott, cutting it free. She stepped back and rubbed her forearms with her hands, exploring the tingling in the muscles there. He stared at her. "Kinna?" Scott said her name slowly, like trying out a foreign language.

Kinna swung around, found Sasha pressing the heels of her hands into her eye sockets, Jad squat down in front of her trying to see her face.

"What? Saw what, Sash?"

"The creature. Cloud. That black mist. Winding through the gravestones, headed straight at us."

Kinna swung around, her skin breaking out in a wave of goosebumps. Scott was turning like a lawn sprinkler. She'd have laughed if Sasha wasn't so shaken by whatever trick her eyes had played on her.

Jad stood up and tried to pull Sasha into his arms, but she shook him off. "Don't! I'm giving the frigging token on my brain stem a chance to catch up to the fact the story is over."

"Screw me for trying to help." Jad threw his hands up. "You sounded like you were having a breakdown or something."

"The fog," Scott said. "Look at the way it swirls and creeps around the tombstones. It's so dark. I would've freaked out too, Sasha, if I saw that right out of the simulation."

"Does the fog have thousands of tiny little rolling eyes, Scott?" Sasha took her hands away from her eyes and blinked rapidly. She did a fast 360-degree scan of the graveyard and stopped to look at the rest of them looking at her. "I know what it was. I'm not saying the thing is out there right now, I'm just saying I *saw* it and it scared the hell out of me."

Kinna, Scott and Jad traded glances. Kinna tipped her chin in Jad's direction and he shook his head and shrugged. She did the chin thing again, tipping her head Sasha's way and Jad rolled his eyes.

"Babe," he said carefully, "I'm not sure what you

mean. You saw it but you didn't see it?" He looked at Sasha sideways, head turned away, braced for backlash.

"Argh!" she exhaled, throwing up her hands. "I mean it wasn't the fog or my eyes playing tricks. It was that smoky, crawling, disgusting thing from the sim. But I know it was just the token screwing with my senses."

"Like a hallucination," Kinna said.

"I guess, if you want to call it that. Brain gone wrong." Sasha tucked her hair behind her ear and Kinna saw her hand was shaking.

"Part of the psychosomatic gift that keeps on giving, I suppose?" Kinna threw the question at Cinn, who hadn't moved from his position at the side of the steel memorial.

"Indeed," he said, inclining his head in acknowledgement. It wasn't Kinna's imagination this time; he was smirking.

"Guys, will we pack it in?" Jad moved to Sasha's side but didn't try to touch her again. "These mind tricks are getting really intense. What if the next one is really strong? Could one of us have a seizure or heart attack or something, if we felt too cold or too hot or…?"

"Too scared?" Cinn finished. "Naturally, the decision to abandon the experience is yours." He sighed and clasped his hands behind his back. "It is unfortunate you will be the first group to not finish the entire suite of simulations."

"Ha!" Scott barked. Kinna seconded it. Cinn's attempt to shame them was so unexpected and blatant, she couldn't keep the sound in. Funnier still, it was working - on her at least. Time enough later to wonder what it said about her that a simulated, glowing, blue man could provoke her. She met Scott's eyes. He raised an eyebrow at her. The muscles in his cheeks were twitching, trying to suppress a smile. He knew she couldn't turn down the challenge. Time enough later to wonder why him knowing her so well made her blush.

"Sash, I don't care if we finish," Jad said. "Say the word, we're out of here. If Chaytor and Mahoney want to stay, I'll give you a piggy-back the whole way home." He took a chance on holding her hand. When she didn't pull away, he brought it to his lips and kissed her knuckles.

Kinna thought she heard Sasha mumble, "Showoff."

"Whatever you want, babe. I think I'm ready to go anyway. My knee hurts where I cut it earlier. And my elbows." He hissed as he bent his free arm.

Sasha shook her head and pressed her lips together. "Jad. I've seen you finish a friendly rugby game with your ear half ripped off and three broken fingers taped together. Don't bullshit me."

"But earlier, you said we should go when I tripped."

"I know! I was being an idiot. You know how I get. You're fine. And I'm fine, too. I don't want to leave. And not because Crypt Keeper over there," she pointed at Cinn, "is pushing us. Getting a scare out of this is kind of the point, isn't it?" She took a deep breath and exhaled hard, her lips vibrating. "What about you two? Do you want to stop here or go on? And why are you being so weird with each other?"

If she was blushing before, Kinna's face caught fire when Sasha called her and Scott out for...what? What did "being weird with each other" look like? Kinna didn't want to be under Sasha's microscope until she'd sat with this new feeling she was having for Scott. Hanging out with him in the cemetery for the rest of the night was the perfect opportunity. Maybe, like, accidentally stumble over a crack in the path and bump up against him, get close enough to catch that spicy scent from his skin again.

"I'm good to keep going," Scott said. "When's the last time you turned down a dare, Kin?"

"Fifth grade," she said.

"And that was only because you wouldn't grab that old cat by the tail and spin him around like Darrin Wilkies dared you to."

"Yeah, but I did take you up on your dare to punch Darrin in the face when he made a grab for the cat."

"So, Kinna's in, is what she's saying," Scott said with a nod.

"Excellent," Cinn said. His map appeared and the group approached for a closer look. A star was spinning at the edge of a large square filled with a uniform pattern of smaller squares, like a checkerboard. "I am delighted you decided to stay. Our next stop offers something unique from the others. It would have been a shame to miss it." The map collapsed as if an imaginary hand folded it. He turned to lead them away. Kinna, Jad and Sasha began to follow.

"Wait. Did Addy come back from her trip to Ichor Peaks?" Scott asked the question as his fingers traced the engraved words on the steel memorial.

"What do you believe, Mr. Mahoney?" Cinn replied.

"Seriously, can you ever just answer a question?"

"I did tell you at the beginning you would have to de-cide—"

"Decide, interpret, guess. Yeah, I remember. It's irritating as hell. I just want to know which Adriana Scala they named the memorial trust for: Granny Adriana or Addy? It's obviously named for whichever one is missing."

"Maybe both of them are missing," Kinna said.

Cinn held his hands wide and shrugged his shoulders, his features set in symmetrical neutrality. He strode away from the memorial, through the chain boundary, and continued along the wide paved path in the direction of their next stop. He turned onto an un-mowed trail.

"It's like he tries to irritate us," Scott said when he reached Kinna's side. They followed behind Jad and Sasha's conjoined shapes, Cinn's phantom blue light guiding them in the distance.

"Look up the answer on your phone," Kinna said, then tried her best imitation of the Investigation Nation host: "A memorial in steel. One name, two women. Join us as the internet reveals their shocking fate!"

"Ha! I would, but my phone's dead."

"I'll check." Kinna's battery was almost gone, too.

"No, leave it. I'll look it up when we get home. If you bury your face in your phone, you'll end up taking a nose-dive like Sir Trips-a-Lot."

"I heard that," Jad said.

"You were supposed to," Scott replied. He stuck his elbow out toward Kinna. She looked at it for a beat, then understood. When she linked her arm with his, she did it slowly, weighted it with intentions she hadn't had when she'd done the same with him earlier in the night. He smiled without looking at her and said, "Besides, I want to focus on this part of the cemetery. Look how different it is from the other parts we've been in."

Kinna took an experimental inhale and caught a whiff of soapy orange. Or was it lemon? She christened it New Scott Smell and grinned as she flicked her flashlight over the tombstones on either side of them. Many of the markers here were short, white rectangular slabs bordered by low concrete walls, little higher than sidewalk curbs. The further down the unkept path they went, the more graves were overgrown with bushes whose kinked, tangled branches hadn't been trimmed in years. Kinna saw at least four broken stones, snapped at jagged angles and tumbled front-forward onto the weeds.

"Nobody has cleaned these up in a long time."

"Over the years, families move, relatives die off, ancestors are forgotten," Cinn called from the head of their procession. "Yet, they are fortunate despite the neglect; their names are still knowable to anyone who might choose to look. Some souls residing here do not have that privilege." He stopped and waved his arm, inviting the group to come forward. Four flashlight beams panned across a compact bed of speckled crushed granite no more than a hundred metres square. The area was filled with small identical wooden crosses. Each had a rectangular metal plate with an inscription. Sasha knelt in front of the nearest cross.

"Unknown Female," she read. She leaned over and flicked her light over a half-dozen of the nearest crosses. "Unknown Female. Unknown Male. Unknown Male. No names on any of them."

"Indeed, Ms. Balakov. This is a potter's field. Final resting place for the nameless. The poor. The disowned."

"Bummer," Jad said.

"That's pretty sad," Sasha said, standing and brushing the knees of her jeans.

"Let me show you one of our anonymous residents."

The group inhaled sharply, as if on cue, as a curtain of black dropped over their eyes.

101

Don't know how I got here. Wherever "here" is. This pink and white quilt definitely isn't mine. And my mattress feels like a sack of baseballs, not a sheet of plywood. These walls? No wallpaper with blue flowers and twisty vines in my bedroom. These nightstands with brass knobs match that dresser against the wall. Ha! I never saw a matching set of furniture in my life.

So, this isn't my bedroom or my bed. What's in those pictures stuck on the dresser mirror? Hard to make out, the light is bad, but looks like some ugly babies. That framed one on its own, a wedding picture, black and white; girl is a real fox in that fifties-movie-star way, but the dude — hope he laid off the potato chips, because that gut was only getting started back then.

Ooh. A jewelry box. Worth a peek. If I can roll outta here...oh, man. I can't even sit up. Why do my arms feel like bags of milk?

"Jesus! You two come from?" Was that my voice? Since when do I croak like that? Maybe if I hack a bit. Gross. Smoke. Ashes. Friggin' Bobby and those bargain cigarettes he sold me. He's getting a fist down his throat when I see him.

Got so caught up casing the place, didn't even see those two at the foot of the bed. An old man and woman. Didn't notice the smell, either. Air's thick with mothballs and something that reminds me of the alley behind Earl's Diner. Sickly sweet, but sharp. Grandparenty couple if ever I saw one, right down to the beige sweater-pants combo on the guy and the flowery apron on the female.

"Don't talk yet, son," the man says. "You breathed in a lot of smoke. Here, take a drink." He holds up a plastic blue cup and sits the straw on my lips. Gotta be careful here; taking things from strangers hasn't been helpful to me any time in my eighteen years. But the back of my throat is so dry it feels crispy. Just a sip, slow, until I'm as sure as I can be that it's only water. God, that's good. I'll take it all, thank you very much.

Granny comes up and sits on the bed. Quite the dip it takes under her fat ass. She picks up my hand and rubs her thumb across my knuckles. I'm getting a good friendly vibe from these two. Might make a mark out of them yet. After I figure out how the hell I ended up in their bedroom.

"You got here a little while ago," says the man, like he fished the question out of my brain. "After they put the fire out."

Breathing smoke. The fire.

He says it and my body heats up like it's dropped in a pot of boiling water. Forget mothballs; only thing I'm smelling now is burning wood and smoke. Can't stop the coughing fit that twists and bends me up. It kills my chest and stomach, hunching up like that. What's that stinging from my left shoulder to my right hip? And my head. My temple throbs – boom, boom, boom – like there's a heart in my head. Take a feel around my skull. Nothing there but the tickly stubble of my brush cut. Damn, it's tender, though, right where it's pounding.

So. A fire. Got this faint memory of blazing orange and yellow all around me. Lying inside a sunset. Blanking on the why and how of it, though. *Think, think, think!* You're not safe 'til you remember.

I've learned a few things these two years on my own. Throw them in with the mad skills I pulled from my year in juvie and I'm a survival machine. First rule: never let anyone have the upper hand. Sometimes that means bluffing, puffing yourself out like a rabid dog to scare people off; sometimes it means showing your belly, making them think you're harmless until you can snatch control. Don't know where I stand with these two. I mean, no doubt I can knock them around if I have to, probably turn the old farts to dust, but I can't see the big picture yet. Why am I here? What happened to me? Could be hallucinating for all I know. Cigarettes aren't the only thing I get off Bobby and some of that crap can give you flashbacks. If I look at two of them long enough, her with that curled-under mop and thick round glasses, him with that horseshoe of white hair and button-up sweater gaping around his fat gut, they got a familiar look. But all old people look the same: hunched, faded, and wrinkled. Used up.

I'll show them my belly.

"How did I get here? What—what happened?" Use the small voice. Everyone buys that. I'm skinny as a light pole and got this pale skin.

"There was a fire. You don't remember?" the woman asks.

The anger flares under my ribs. Would I ask if I remembered, you old bag? It's not time yet, but I'm gonna like watching her shrink away when I start yelling in her face and shake everything in her jewelry box into a pillowcase.

"A fire, yes. My throat. The smoke." Clear my throat. Sell it. "But where?"

The man looks at the woman and shrugs, nods. She covers my hand. It's pinned between two of hers now. So cold. What's with old people being like ice cubes?

"It was in an apartment building. Low-rise at Javelin and Summerville. Oh! I think he remembers, George." The wife pats my hand. Dammit. I gave it away. Couldn't keep the surprise off my face. The apartment, the streets. I do remember. And I know damn well why I was there.

Javelin and Summerville was a stick-up job. Earl usually hands me my gigs, but I went independent on that one. Stuff to prove. To Earl, his crew. Myself. Ha! Look at me now, Earl! Lying in an old folks' bed, being looked after by a couple of fossils. Hard to keep a lid on this laugh, can't tell a lie.

It was better when I didn't remember. Now I know I got a problem. Earl's gonna find out I tried to do a job on my own. Earl doesn't like solo acts. I've been working for him a couple of years. He spotted me stomping on the pills of a flash-dressed asshat who was stupid enough to stop right in the middle of the sidewalk to count the wad of cash he pulled out of the ATM. Thank you very much, I took that invitation, and beat him to the concrete before he got to his Cadillac. Earl waited for me to come out of the alley, walked up and clapped me on the back. Looked like Tony Soprano or Kingpin when he took that chomped-up cigar out of his mouth and said, "Kid, I like your attitude. How'd you like a job?" I knew who Earl Bryant was; nobody said no to Earl. That's why he didn't wait for an answer, just laughed, slapped me on the back again and steered me down the street to the diner he owned.

Earl had an idea, see. A vision, he called it. A group of young swellies he could send on jobs where his clumsy thick-necked bruisers would give themselves away. He guinea pigged me. Got me dressed up in one of them collared t-shirts the rich douchebags on Quay Street wear and nasty beige pants all pleated in the front. Sent me on dentist appointments to scope out where they kept the drugs. He'd send his trolls in after hours to break out the good stuff. Even got myself a wisdom tooth pulled and a couple of fillings out of it. Send me into any swank neighbourhood with Earl's wife's Pekepoo on a leash and I could case any house, any car, without getting a second look. Shrank my balls to be seen walking that rat dog, but the payout made up for it. Earl put money in my pocket and proved me right for dropping school and ditching my baby-factory mother. He got me street smart. But I got sick of the swelly routine. Needed more action. And he wouldn't give it to me. So, I decided to take it. I was done learning from him. That's what I told myself when the lightbulb went off about the apartment building on Javelin and Summerville.

Old dude and the lady are staring at me. Sure, folks, I remember what happened in that building. Everything except how I got from there to here. But they don't need to know. Not until I want them to know, need them good and scared and babbling not to hurt them. Just gonna pull my hand free of hers, get my other one out on top of the quilt. Start getting ready.

"Yeah," I say. "The apartment building. It was on fire." Shuffle a few cards around in the old noggin here, see which one I should play, settle on, "I saw it from the street. Place was going up fast. Someone was on the sidewalk freaking out about people inside. I went in to help get them out."

Missus blinks at me through her pop-bottle glasses. Can't say I expect the laugh that rips out of her. Just the kind of jiggly sound you'd expect out of your fat grandmother. Mister frowns at her and she tries to shut it down behind a hand, but it's pushing out between her fingers. Did I play the wrong card? "It was a bad fire, too," the old man says. "They're pretty sure it was started on purpose."

I don't like the sound of that. Fire department shouldn't be on to it so quick. I made it look like an accident for chrissakes.

"You're very brave," granny says. "Did you get anybody out of there, dear?"

She still looks like she wants to laugh. Time comes, she'll be getting the first punch, right in that mouth. Relax those hands, now, son. Not ready for fists. Not yet. The game's changed. Let's find out what they know, catch those flies with honey. Two of them'll have strokes if I try to beat it out of them.

"No, I couldn't save anyone." Swallow hard, rub your

hands together a bit. You're sooo sad about it. God, I'm golden at this. "I got into the lobby and got to the second floor, where the fire was. I heard screaming behind one of the doors. Kicked it in, but the whole place was burning. Even the ceiling. Heat hit me flat in the face, hot enough to burn the hair off you. I got a few feet inside. Bit hazy, but it was too hot. I think I tried to go back. Rest is a total blank." Propane caught too fast, seems like. Blew before I made it out. Piece of crap stove; worthless as everything else in that apartment. Hopefully there wasn't much left of that moron I left in there.

Man, my chest and stomach. Felt that earlier, but the sting and itch is really ramping up. If I can just get myself up a bit, really give it a scratch. Why the hell can't I sit up? Oh man, did I break my back? No. No, wait. You can move your arms, idiot. Weak as these two geezers, though. Get those hands back in under the quilt, under the t-shirt. Oh, yeah. Dig those nails in. Won't stop itching, though. Stings, too. Sweating like a beast here. Figures these two'd keep their heat turned up to incinerate.

"Be patient, it'll come back to you," missus says. "You were lucky. I can't say as much for others in the building. A shame what happened there." Bugger looks me dead in the eye. "Shame."

She getting at something? Screw you old lady. Even if she is, not like it was my fault. The dumbass in that apartment should've known better than to make himself a target.

I ran drugs to one of Earl's dealers on Javelin at least once a week. About a month ago, I saw a skinny guy in an old-style gangster hat go into the apartment building on the corner carrying a black metal briefcase. The way he leaned to one side told me it had some weight to it. Wasn't that got me eyeballing it, though. It was the handcuffs. Anyone who cuffed a case to his wrist like that had something worth keeping inside it. And shifty eyes? This guy swept the street around him like he was taking a broom to it. I started to keep an eye out for him. Next time I saw him, I waited around for him to leave again. He came out with the case still cuffed, but I could tell by the way he walked it was lighter. Maybe empty. So, whatever he had, he dropped inside that building. Started watching him on purpose, then. Got to know his habits. Figured out what apartment he was in. Didn't see any muscle guarding the place. Made a plan.

I coulda told Earl about it. Was going to, but that bobo Larry was due for the next job and I didn't want Earl saddling me with one of the older guys. Larry'd think he was in charge. This was *my* job, start to end. Earl didn't need to know. Or need a cut.

Picked my night and waited for the guy to show up. He was usually in and out in thirty minutes when he did the drops. I gave him ten minutes and made my way up to the second floor, knocked on his door. I'd put on my fancy douchey clothes like Earl taught me. Took some convincing to get the guy to believe I was there to check the gas connections in the building. He shuffled around a bit on the other side and finally unlocked four locks on the door. Four! I couldn't wait to see what this guy was stashing.

My nose tried to turn itself inside-out from the smell of pure vinegar inside. Had to rub the water out of my eyes, too. He had a cloth balled up in his hand, like he'd been cleaning. How do you stand it, I asked him? Dude narrowed his eyes at me out of his skinny ferret face and told me to get to my business checking the gas line in the kitchen. I dragged my heels, making small talk. What was his name? What did he do? Gave me a minute to scope out the apartment. Know what I found? Books. Stacks and stacks of books. On every table, every chair, every corner of the floor. I leaned on a stack to hold myself still so I could tippy-toe a look deeper into the room, but the stack slipped sideways under my hand and slid across the floor. He sucked in air like I'd given him a smack in the guts and flapped his hands around his face. Out! Out! Out! He yelled it like he had a choice in me coming or going.

I walked over the avalanche of paper, shook his hand off my arm when he tried to grab me. I spotted the brief-case on a tiny TV tray in the living room, top flipped open. Well. When I saw the books inside it, can't tell a lie, sweet hot rage filled me up. Dropped the act altogether then. I shoved my way through the books between me and that case. Threw 'em from one end of the room to the other. Ferret Face jumped on my back. I whipped my elbow back and got him right in his guts. Slid off me and crumbled to the floor. I hauled him up by the front of his hair and screamed in his face to tell me where the good stuff was. Guy was a crackpot. He babbled something, drool dribbled down his chin. Useless. I rammed my fist into his eye socket to shut him up and dropped him. Last ditch, I grabbed a couple of books out of the briefcase and turned them upside down, flicking the pages on the off chance there were surprises inside. Empty. Of course. The books themselves might've been special. How would I know?

Wasn't anyone I could offload them on in my world any-way. That was it. Not a cent to be made on this job.

It was a bad time for him to make a sound. His little girl whimper set me off inside. People talk about seeing red? It's honest to God a real thing. I don't remember everything I said, but the gist was he'd wasted my time. Hauled him up off the floor again and shook him by the front of his shirt like I was trying to get a stuck candy bar out of a vending machine. His teeth clacked together. I don't know if I let him go, or if the front of his shirt tore or what, but next thing he was stumbling away from me, tripped, and brought his head down on the corner of the heavy wood coffee table poking out of the towers of books. He never moved a muscle. That isn't what you want: robbing a place is one thing, having some nutter die on you is another. That's real jail time. I squat next to him and jammed my fingers under his jaw but couldn't find a heartbeat.

I stayed there for a minute and asked myself what Earl would do. Sweat dripped down my face and soaked my armpits bad enough I could smell myself over the vinegar. The pit smell brought me back to the Brookfield Bakery fire a few months back, where me and Larry, him stinking like a wet sheep, did a torch job. A fast burn through this guy's apartment would cover off everything. Fingerprints. The body. Kicked my way through the worthless books and eyed bucko's propane stove. I opened the valves on the burners.

Couldn't just throw a match in there. Place would blow. Time. I needed time to get out and away. Far away.

Down the hall I found a bathroom — everything but

the toilet filled with books, of course. The stack in the clos-
et was dry as unbuttered toast and caught on my first try.
Whoosh! I bolted for the apartment door. Idea was the fire
would take long enough to reach the gas I'd be long gone
when they got together and boom-boomed. That was the
plan, anyway.

"But that wasn't what happened, was it?"

My head whips around to pops. "Hell you say?"
Head's throbbing again. What's that tickle? Blood? I'm
bleeding out my temple.

"You didn't make it to the door," he says. "Herschel
stopped you."

"What the f—"

"He wasn't dead," the old bag interrupts. "Herschel
caught you from behind, pulled you down by the cuff of
your pants, and you cracked your head on the same table
you'd smashed his on."

"I didn't smash his head, he *fell!*" I don't mean to
say it. Floods out with the anger cracking through me as
my memory snaps to life and forces me to remember *he*
stopped me. Herschel, the useless ferret-faced turd.

But feels good to use my normal voice on these two
and give 'em a yell. No more showing the belly. They figured out the game. Time to puff myself up and show the
teeth. Can't say these two are smart, though. Not even a
flinch when I roared at 'em. That's fine, when I get my
hands around their turkey necks, that'll change. Goddamn it, why can't I sit up? Like there's a boulder on my
chest. The heat! Gotta get this blanket off me. Christ! My
hand! Was that a sizzle?

Old man picks up the story. "Those books burned a lot

faster than you thought they would." His wife nods her stupid head. She's not trying to hide her smile anymore. Cocky bitch. Smart enough to move out of arm's reach, though.

The weight on my chest. I can't breathe. And the heat! That's not it. Not heat. It's burning. The blanket is burning down into my chest. My legs. "What is this? What do you want?" This…it's not happening. Close my eyes here, try to suck in some air.

Smoke? Where…what's burning? Where'd the old-timers go? Can barely see them through the haze. God help me, the heat. The wallpaper, it's curling off the walls. My arms won't move anymore.

"A lot of people live in an apartment building. But you didn't care about that when you cranked up that gas and tried to burn Herschel alive."

Don't know who's saying what. The pounding in my head. I can't concentrate. It's one voice. They're speaking at the same time? An echo.

"We lived in the apartment above Hershel. He kept mostly to himself, but if you got him in the right mood, he'd talk and talk about those books and typewriters of his – did you see the typewriters? He was always coming and going with them. Such a quiet man. We liked that. Didn't keep us awake at night. We were asleep the night you stopped by to see him. You know, we didn't even wake up with all that ruckus you were causing. They said the smoke got us first. Before we burned. In our bed."

The room is an oven. If I could just get my legs free. Okay. Calm down. CALM DOWN! Everything itches. Stomach's the worst. Can't scratch it. Can't…oh no, no it's bad. Shit! Forgot the blanket is hot. Why is it hot? Can't scratch.

"Oh, yes. Your stomach. That's where the beam landed. The smack on the head didn't kill you, you see. It only knocked you out. You stayed alive long enough for the whole place to catch fire and fall apart. The beam hit you and you came to. Pinned you long enough so you could feel the burn."

Am I remembering, or are they putting memories in my head? I can't tell. I just feel. Scorching. My whole body. The itch bursting into a flaming burn crawling across my skin. The blanket's smoking.

"Herschel made it out. He never told the firemen to check his apartment. Who can blame him? It was too late for you by then anyway."

Herschel got out? Bad. The cops know. Earl. It's too late. Too late. Wait. "Wait. Too late for me?" Hard to force the words out.

"No matter how many times we do this, you never remember."

I'm shaking. Can't scream. Voice almost gone. My skin. A glance at my hand. A bubble on my palm. The skin stretching and swelling, filling with liquid. My God, the pain. It won't stop. More. All over hands, arms. *Pop. Pop-pop. Pop.* Bursting. Liquid runs. Spits and hisses on my searing flesh. Shiny and pink. Those red strands. Muscle.

"Look at you! Peeling open like an onion. At least the smoke got us first."

Can't think.

"Yes, Hershel got out. You, on the other hand. You stayed under that beam. Trapped. Nobody to help you.

Just...burning."

Flames. Licking like snake tongues. Through the quilt. Didn't think I could scream. Shreds the inside of my throat. Blackness is coming. Please. Yes.

"Uh-uh." Voice comes with a slap across my face. Oh, God. They're back. Staring at me. At the foot of the bed. "Not yet. You're not done. You always try to leave at this part."

Always?

"There it is, Helen. The look. That's right, boy. You've been here before."

"We were so nervous when this all started, remember George?" she says back to him. "And you?" Her finger's a knife in my chest. "You bullied us. Tried it all. You made it all the way out of the building the first few times. But we have the hang of it now. This is our favourite, when you think you're getting one over on us."

"How...long?" All I can choke out. My cheeks and lips split open. I can't...

"How long have you been here? Time is different here. What do you think, Helen?"

"Oh, I don't know. We've been through this a good many times now, George. Seventy? Eighty?"

"Closer to 100 I'd say."

"Let's call it 100 even, then."

End's close. Please, God.

"Tsk-tsk. Helen, he still doesn't get it. Boy, it doesn't end. You died in that building. Alone. A twisted, crackling corpse. Nobody knew your name. Nobody came to claim you. Just us."

The pain. It's everywhere.

"Oh, George! I have a great idea for 101."

6

"I'm hot," Kinna said. "Like, really, really hot. Is anyone else?" The others shook their heads. Kinna pulled the collar of her shirt away from her throat with a finger and jerked. "Ouch! My skin is super sensitive too."

"Here, let me see." Scott closed in and was sizing up the skin on her neck before she could react. His warm breath huffed against her throat. She shivered as if someone had sent an electric current sizzling through her body.

"Stop. Too much." She slapped his hands away and took a step back.

"Sorry! Sensitive. I get it."

Kinna fumbled to open her jacket, fluffed the front of her shirt to force air down the neck, across her chest.

"I love a good revenge story," Sasha said.

"You would, bloodthirsty minx," Jad said, earning a jab in the ribs. Then, to the group, "Can anyone else smell smoke?"

Scott inhaled and swallowed twice, quickly. "More like cooked meat."

"Me too," Sasha said. "You heard it here first: I'm now a vegetarian."

"So nobody knows who that guy was?" Kinna asked Cinn, fanning herself. "He just turned up dead in a fire and they put him here?"

"Coroner reports and eye-witness accounts attest to his cause of death and criminal intentions, but, of course, the rest is—"

"—up to you to decide," Jad said, doing his best Percivet Cinn impression. "Who can say for sure the man isn't being eternally tortured in the bowels of hell for his sins! Moohoohahaha!"

Sasha burst out laughing. Scott smiled, keeping his lips tight and the contents of his stomach on lock-down.

"Do you not tire of being the court jester, Mr. Erim?" Cinn asked. A series of ripples passed through his shape, briefly erasing the definition of his face and bending his limbs at jagged angles.

"Ah, did you guys see that?" Kinna asked.

"What?" Scott said, looking around. "If you saw a crispy zombie out there, tell me right now."

"No," Kinna said, but couldn't help glancing between the tombstones. "No, Cinn's shape went screwy."

"I didn't see anything," Sasha said.

"Did you, Jad? Maybe it was just my token," Kinna said, feeling it with her fingers. "My skin's so damn hot it's probably frying it. Hello, Jad?" Kinna waved her hand in front of Jad's fixed stare.

Sasha snapped her fingers in front of him and shouted, "Hey!" She tapped him on the cheek with her hand.

Jad's eyelids fluttered. His eyes focused and his head nodded. He looked at Sasha. "Huh? What did you say?"

"That was freaky, man," Scott said. "What happened?"

"What happened when?" Jad said slowly, still blinking up a storm.

"Ah, when you went space cadet for about thirty seconds just then?" Sasha said.

"Nothing. I was speaking, then you were slapping me in the face."

"I didn't slap you, I tapped you after you went blank, staring into nothing."

Jad opened his mouth and shut it, shook his head.

"Can the tokens make you phase out like that?" Kinna asked Cinn, rubbing hers again. It felt like it was vibrating.

"The Virtokens are tested, calibrated, and tested again before every use, Ms. Chaytor."

"I didn't ask you that, I asked you if it could happen."

"It is not a known side-effect of the Virtoken, no." Cinn turned to Jad. "Some types of seizures are known to manifest in this manner. Do you suffer from epilepsy Mr. Erim?"

"For God's sake! No, I don't have seizures. If I did zone out, so what? Forgive a guy for taking a second to appreciate the human scum barbeque we just watched. Stop fussing like a bunch of old ladies." Jad shooed the others, including Cinn, further down the path. He looked around, then stopped. Pointed at Cinn. "Roll out the map, Jedi ghost, and show us where we're going. I'm fine! Shushie!" The last was directed at Sasha, who'd inhaled like she was going to speak.

"Certainly," Cinn said, inclining his head. He waved

his hands and revealed the map. One spinning star remained, near the centre of the cemetery.

"One more to go," Jad said. "Perfect. Wicked." He started walking.

"I don't know if I'm disappointed or relieved it's almost done," Kinna said. Her body was cooling off, but in its wake her skin started to itch.

"Probably best it's close to finished," Sasha said. She looked at Jad's broad back as if trying to pierce it with her eyes. "Someone's getting cranky."

"I'm hungry!" Jad said, flinging his arms wide.

Scott clamped his lips together and sucked air deep into his lungs.

"Gonna be okay?" Kinna asked, coming up beside him as they followed Jad down the path.

"How can he think about food after seeing that?" Scott said and buttoned his lips again.

"Jad ate a slug off the ground one time for twenty bucks, Scott. Just roll with it. Oh, sorry." Scott had stopped, his Adam's apple bobbing convulsively. "That sim really grossed you out, hey?"

"It didn't bother you?" he said.

"No, not really. I didn't get the smell the way you guys did."

Sasha blew by them, almost clipping Kinna on the way, and marched to Jad's side. Kinna looked over her shoulder. Percivet Cinn was float-walking ten feet behind them. Kinna caught his lips moving before he flicked his eyes up and fixed a toothy smile on his face.

"I've been getting a weird vibe from him after the last couple of sims," she said.

"The sarcasm, you mean? Yeah, they should change that part of the program. I don't mind so much, but it would turn some people off."

"The sarcasm is part of it, yeah. But more. Like, he gets annoyed." Kinna listed examples from the night, ending with Jad making fun of Cinn, the way Cinn's image had flickered and distorted right as Jad spaced out.

"You think Cinn did something to Jad? That's a reach, Kinna. They'd build safeguards into the programming to prevent it."

"Are you kidding me right now? Have you heard of HAL 9000? *2001: A Space Odyssey? The Matrix? I, Robot?*"

Scott sighed. "Obviously. Those are stories, though." Scott glanced past Kinna to see Cinn float by them, his shape bending and folding as he skimmed through the headstones in his way. He overtook Jad and Sasha, who had stopped at the intersection of two trails. The two turned left to follow him.

"How about the *Titanic*? Heard of that one? Engineers make mistakes, Scott. That's all I'm saying."

"Look." Scott motioned down the path to a glowing blue shape in the fog. Two flashlight beams were swinging around it. "We're almost there. One and done." His eyes flicked over her shoulder. His scream was ear-splitting.

Kinna screamed automatically, spinning, her heart galloping. Eight black-shrouded figures stood in the mist, hoods pulled low to cover their faces. Between them they supported the weight of a door-sized slab of rock, its edges carved with Gothic script. Atop it lay a man in knight's armour, arms crossed over his chest. The entire tomb shuffled and swayed as the fog ebbed and flowed around the stone pallbearers and the effigy they carried on their shoulders.

"What happened? Are you guys okay?" Sasha's voice, distant, reached Kinna through the blood rushing in her ears.

"Yes, we're fine," Scott called back, panting. "I just shit my pants is all."

"Saw the spooks in the cloaks, did ya?" Jad shouted. "Percy said some rich guy had it made for himself, copied it off an old tomb somewhere in France."

"Right on," Scott called back. He said to Kinna, "I can't wait to get out of here. I'm going to have a heart attack."

Kinna rubbed her chest, over her heart. "Yeah. Me too. Come on." She took Scott by the hand and met his eyes, looking at him from under her eyelashes. He frowned for a second, then his lips opened slightly in surprise. She smiled and tugged on his hand to pull him down the path with her. After a moment, he squeezed her fingers and rubbed his thumb across hers. By the time they arrived in the circle of light created by Cinn and Jad and Sasha's lights, Scott's face was split in a smile.

"Oh, that's how it is, is it?" Jad said. "You're gonna look like that forever if the wind changes, you know."

"Finally," Sasha added. "The pheromones flying around for the last hour were making me dizzy."

"Shuddup," Kinna mumbled, her blush coming back for an encore. Scott's smile widened.

"Ah, love," Cinn said. "So precious."

"You manage to make everything sound creepy, Percy," Sasha said. Jad's face lit up when she used the nickname and he offered her his hand for a high-five. She gave it a perfect slap without looking.

Cinn closed his eyes. His expression was that of a man who'd caught the scent of lumpy sour milk. "Percivet. Why is your generation so completely lacking in manners?"

"Why don't we get this over with, then?" Kinna said to him. She'd started losing interest in the end of the simulation the minute she took Scott's hand. She wanted to be anywhere else. With him. Alone. "We can go home and you can go to whatever cyber-void you go when you aren't insulting and baiting guests in graveyards."

Cinn opened his eyes and sighed. "Cemetery."

"What?" Kinna said.

"It is called a cemetery. It is a graveyard when it adjoins a church."

"Oh, for the love of God," Sasha said, throwing up her hands. "Give the attitude a rest."

Cinn pulled at the bottom of his waistcoat to straighten it and pushed his hands back through his hair to flatten the pieces that had escaped his slick cap of hair. It was the first time all night Kinna noticed his programmed appearance was anything other than immaculate.

"It is interesting you use that term, Ms. Balakov," Cinn said. "Restlessness is a theme in our next story." He motioned to a polished grey rectangular stone standing knee-high on his right. The name *Sulva* was engraved across the back in scripted letters. The epitaph was on its opposite side, hidden from view. "Are you ready, children?"

"Not children," Kinna heard Jad say before her senses blanked.

DARLING

It was just my mom and I after Dad died. No grand-parents, godparents, cousins. It *should've* been me and Mom against the world.

Our family had moved around a lot before the accident. Dad was an orderly trained to work in institutions for the criminally insane. Not many people wanted the work, so there were always jobs, he could dictate his terms, and the pay was great. My parents would keep an eye out for fixer-upper houses in places near the type of hospitals Dad worked in, moving there at the end of the school year. Dad earned the cash, Mom renovated the place they'd bought and, when they were ready to move on, they'd sell it for a profit and we'd go to a new city or town.

Me making friends and getting good grades was too conventional for my parents; they said they were giving me an education of the world by bringing me to new places and making me meet reams of new people.

"Darling, cliques and dating and sports are so *bougie*," my mom said when I asked in tenth grade if we could stay a while in Santa Vestos because I made an actual friend.

Taking a drag off her joint, she asked, "Why do you want to be like everyone else? You get to be totally unique." Mom, with her ripped jean overalls and bell sleeve floral shirts, didn't understand that totally unique was totally impractical for a teenager.

But I did all right. Most schools were the same, most of the kids in them a version of ones I'd met before. Jocks and geeks, cheerleaders and choir birds. The ones who wanted to disappear, the ones who wanted to be noticed. If I played it right, I could find the sweet spot where the groups butted-up against each other, but never overlapped. The no man's land of social interactions where you could see everyone but be separate from them. This strategy got me safely through high school without a single wedgie or bitch-slap. No kisses or feel-ups, either, but it felt like a fair trade. If I started to feel a twinge of loneliness, I'd go for a mental soak in a bookstore or library.

Reading was a miracle tonic and horror was my drug of choice. My first hit was when I found *Tales for the Midnight Hour* in my elementary school library. "The Furry Collar" made me sleep with the lights on for a week. Hard to relax when all you can think of is a girl finding the walking corpse of her decapitated friend scratching at her bedroom door. J.B. Stamper was my soul sister through all of sixth grade. I cranked the scare-factor each year, until I hit the likes of Stephen King, Anne Rice, Dean Koontz. Between new releases, I read the classics: Poe, Shelley, Jackson, Bradbury. My sweetest fix? Vampire novels. Modern takes didn't do it for me. But any night after I read the originals - *Dracula, The Vampyre, Carmilla,* and their bed fellows - I'd fall asleep imagining the pressure of those sharp teeth against the soft skin of my neck or wrist. Piercing. The flow of warm wet blood as the vampire's long cool body pressed against me. I got worried at one point I had a weird fixation. Turned out that even if I was a deviant, I was in good company. Sexy vampire fantasies were *everywhere* in the early 1980s according to *People Magazine* and the popularity of that Dracula movie with Laurence Olivier that came out a few years ago.

But that was the old me. The me before the accident. Before Rhys.

My dad died in 1983. He'd gotten a one-year contract with the Waterton Regional Hospital. My parents bought a ranch-style fixer-upper near the city's downtown. I enrolled in Waterton Community College's Computer Science program (computers were *Time Magazine*'s newsmaker of the year in 1982; I figured if I worked with them I'd have a portable skill set to keep bouncing around with Mom and Dad).

When I was younger, we'd arrive in a new place and I'd think, *This is it! This is the time Dad's hospital will be called something cool, like Institute for the Criminally Insane, or Hospital for the Perpetually Mental.* It never happened. I understood why these places deserved to have respectful names, but I still felt letdown when I saw boring old Waterton Regional Hospital on Dad's contract.

My disappointment was short-lived. Within days, my father was telling us stories about WRH unlike any from the other place he'd worked.

WRH was a legit nineteenth-century building, complete with basement cells made with sweaty stone walls. They moved some patients down there from the top floor in the summer when it got too hot and the winter when it got too cold. Some patients didn't react well to being locked in the little dark rooms. There was one girl who'd been institutionalized after she'd killed her sister because she thought big sis was an alien imposter. She was in a basement cell when her meds started to kick in and the slow realization of what she'd done hit her. She cracked her skull slamming it against the stone wall before anyone could stop her. Oh, and there was the serial rapist who cut off his own you-know-what with a shard of rock because he got the idea one of the insects lurking in the corner of his cell had crawled up into it.

A lot of people would say my dad shouldn't have been telling these stories to anyone – patient confidentiality and all that - let alone a seventeen-year-old, but my parents never treated me like a kid. I was making breakfast at twelve when Dad had to work back-to-back shifts and Mom was up to her elbows in plaster. I picked up groceries by myself when I was fourteen and walked the five blocks home. I didn't mind. It was special; part of what made us our own unit. It's not like I had anyone I'd repeat the stories to. And it wasn't like there was anything he could tell me that fiction hadn't already prepared me for.

Three months into his contract, Dad was at work one night and they had an inmate, or I guess you'd call him a patient, down in the basement who started screaming and yanking on the bars of his cell – his room? – and ramming his shoulder into them like he was trying to beat them down. The six-foot-six beast was bleeding all over the place. When Rhys told me and Mom about it weeks later, gave us the details the police and hospital administration wouldn't, I'd find out the guy had done his wife and kids in a multiple murder. They'd arrested him sitting at his kitchen table with his family slumped over the table next to him. I remember the way my skin crawled on my scalp when Rhys got to that part; it was the furthest thing I could imagine from the safe, loving family I'd grown up in.

Anyway, they'd brought this guy to WRH after his trial, months before my dad arrived. He'd been catatonic since the verdict was read in court. And then *snap!* He woke up this night, screaming like a banshee, throwing himself around the room. I would've let him keep on pinballing until he'd knocked himself out, or worse. The guy deserved it after what he'd done. But my dad would never do that. He told me and Mom all the time: his job was to help the patients, not judge them. He didn't get angry at me when I rolled my eyes, just told me, "Sometimes the right thing to do doesn't always feel right."

Was he thinking about that when he and two other orderlies, including Rhys, were standing outside the guy's room with a syringe full of sedatives? Or when he saw the patient figure out what was about to happen and the guy stood in the middle of his cell, feet planted, head down, blood pouring into his eyes from his head wound, pumping his arms like a boxer? When Dad and the orderlies pulled a mattress out of storage and gathered behind it single-file in front of the cell door, was Dad thinking it felt wrong, but it was the right thing to do? Dad unlocked the door. They burst in with the mattress between them and the patient and used their momentum to slam him back into the wall and pin him there. That was the idea, at least. They slammed him as planned, but there was too much momentum and my dad stumbled out of the group as they hit the wall. The rest of them lost their footing and everyone fell into a heap on the floor. The orderly with the syringe jabbed it into the guy's arm where it was pinned for a crucial few seconds between the tangle of body parts. As it took effect, the giant got quiet. It was a minute before the others started to peel off the pile. Rhys noticed that my dad had gone quiet, too, and when they got a clear look at him, they saw his head was twisted the wrong way.

I was calm when the phone woke me up at six o'clock in the morning and my mom answered and her voice from the next room got louder and louder until she was screaming, "What do you mean, dead? Dead? DEAD?" I stayed calm when I sat straight up in the bed and ran into her bedroom, almost breaking my pinky toe when I stubbed it on a box full of tiles she'd bought to put down in the bathroom, and sat down next to her and took the phone out of her hand and told the officer to repeat everything she'd just told my mother while Mom cried, slobber and snot all over the shoulder of my t-shirt. I was still calm after I hung up the call and put the phone back in the cradle and folded my other arm around my mother while I stared at the drywall she'd exposed when she started peeling off the foil butterfly wallpaper yesterday.

I wish I could say my calm streak lasted.

Turns out reading horror might prepare you for hearing about awful things that happen to other people – the ones "over there", who you never have to see or meet – but it doesn't help when those things happen to you. Mom had been up late the night before and I guessed she'd taken a few puffs at bedtime to help her relax, so she literally cried herself to sleep on my shoulder after hearing my dad was dead. I couldn't go back to sleep, so I went to make myself a cup of tea. Filled the kettle, put it on the stove. Pulled out a slice of white bread and slathered peanut butter on it. The kettle worked itself up to a shrill whistle and I found myself staring at it, eating the bread. I didn't know I was going to swipe the kettle off the stove with my bare hand and send it flying against the wall. It just happened. Like the scorching burn on my palm. Like the bubbling blisters on my bare feet after the boiling water from the kettle sprayed them. A wave of dizziness crashed down on me and I sat on the floor (honestly, it was more like a fall) shaking and sweating. My mother found me there, curled on my side, sobbing from a pain so deep inside me, I can't believe my heart didn't rip itself open and bleed out with the tears.

I didn't have to overnight at the hospital, thank God. Being in the emergency room, the antiseptic smell and wailing moans from a poor creature a couple of gurneys over, was a visceral reminder of all things Dad. Me and Mom linked our hands together for the two hours I had to lie there and talked about school and renovations and movies and the election; anything to avoid stumbling into the bomb crater left in our lives by that 6am phone call.

I fell full-on into it afterward.

Besides leaving the house for the funeral a sunny morning two days later (me, Mom, and a guy from the local funeral home handing us an urn, offering us greatest sympathies for our loss), I stayed in my room for a month. I didn't go to classes. Barely ate. I cried. I started journaling, then gave it up when I flipped back through the passages and noticed I'd begun to end them all by writing "I don't know what to do" over and over again.

Mom? I wish I could tell you how she dealt with it those first few weeks. My head was buried so far up my own misery she could've moved out and I wouldn't have noticed, except for the one time each day she came to my door, knocked, and asked, "Darling, can I come in?" I wouldn't answer, but would move around so she'd know I was alive. When I heard her footsteps go down the hall, I'd crack the door and reach out like a hand from the damp soil of a grave for the plate of food she'd left for me. Rinse, repeat. The house was mid-renovation when Dad died, but I didn't hear the knock of a hammer or the swish of a paint roller or scrape of a grout trowel for weeks. She must've felt so alone. She was in a new city where she didn't know anyone, with a kid who hardly talked to her anymore, her husband and best friend dead without any warning or expectation. If I hadn't been so selfish, if I'd been more willing to share the grief, I wonder if she would've been less receptive to Rhys when he showed up?

The doorbell rang one evening about a month after the accident. That was weird in and of itself, since we knew pretty much nobody in Waterton. I got up from doodling distorted gravestones in my journal and peaked through the closed blinds on my bedroom window. The front step was hidden by the eve, but there was a red Corvette pulled up to the curb. I heard the front door open, my mother's soft drawl, and a deep muffled voice. I opened my door a crack to find out what new and terrible news this person's visit must be bringing. My room was down the hall, and I had a direct line of sight to the front door. Mom was tall, like me, but this man was a head over her. Lean through his blue-jean wrapped hips, but broad shouldered under his brown leather jacket. The black t-shirt under it matched his side-swept hair and set off the pale cast of his skin. My face and other parts less mentionable warmed up as if someone had turned up the thermostat. My mother stood aside and invited him into the living room. I caught her checking her reflection in the mirror next to the door, tucking her hair here, fluffing it there. When she saw me (who'd barely emerged from my room for four weeks) enter the living room a minute later and sit in our rocking chair, her jaw dropped so far, she could've caught ping-pong balls.

Hello, Rhys. Nice to meet you.

He took the beer my mom offered him and sat on the couch. "I know the hospital has been tight-lipped about David's death," he said. Hearing him say Dad's name was like having a bell rung inside my head. He'd always been Dad, your father, your husband, honey. Using his given name and saying he was dead added a fresh layer of realization to the loss. "I thought you both deserved to know what happened," Rhys continued. That's how we got the full story. The hospital would only say he died in an accident. Mom hadn't been able to get her hands on an official report. We didn't have money for lawyers and hospitals are fortresses of silence; they protect themselves and their own when they catch the faintest whiff of a possible lawsuit. The story Rhys told us pulled back a particularly heavy and painful veil. "It was, you know, kind of heroic, I guess." Rhys ran a hand through his hair and shook his head.

"David was like that," Mom said, wiping away her tears with the back of her hand. "Always believed in the work. Always talking about how vulnerable those people were." I looked between her and Rhys. What the hell was I hearing? Heroic to have your neck broken trying to keep a mass murderer from harming himself? And my mother never referred to "those people" with anything other than the deepest suspicion when my father had talked about them at home: "Half of them probably have the doctors fooled into thinking they weren't in their right minds when they did those horrific things." Mom was a bit of a flower child, but she was no fool.

The liquid crap flooding the room cooled the warmth I'd felt when I first caught sight of Rhys. While he spoke to my mother, I took experimental glances at him; if I stared too long at his long, pale fingers, or the sharp cheekbones under his so-brown-they're-almost-black eyes, the heat kicked up again. If I focused only on what they were saying, it was easier to keep my irritation fresh and stoked.

And it wanted stoking.

What was my mother doing? The way she stared at him when he looked away, shifted on the chair cushion. Rhys was no better. He raked her with his eyes when she had a small crying jag over contract employees like Dad never having insurance or survivor benefits.

If either of them found my glares annoying or unusual, they never said. I may as well have been standing outside a snow globe, looking in at the drifting plastic flakes and tiny figures inside, for all the attention they paid me. Even when I stood to leave and shoved the rocking chair so hard it hit the wall behind me, my mother gave me little more than a lifted eyebrow. I didn't check to see if Rhys looked. From my room, I heard the front door open and shut about an hour later. Ten-o-eight pm.

The next morning, I found my mother sitting at the kitchen table, staring into a bowl of cereal she was slowly stirring with her spoon. "What were you guys talking about for so long?" I wanted her to jump when I asked the question. Gotcha! It was the first breakfast I'd shown up for since the accident and she wasn't expecting me. But she only looked up from the mush of bran in her bowl and smiled.

"Good morning, darling. You're up for breakfast. Did you want some orange juice?"

I narrowed my eyes and repeated my question.

"We just chatted. Rhys told me about some cool places in the city you and I could visit. There's an independent bookstore over on Cairo Drive he thought you might like. I told him what a bookworm you are."

"You chatted? About shopping? After he told you my father broke his neck in a cell in the basement of the hospital?" The pitch of my voice rose on each word until I knew I was almost yelling by the end of it.

Mom dropped the spoon against the bowl.

"Excuse me for having my first real conversation with another human being in over a month. I have a lot to figure out about our future and it helps talking to someone else about it. It's not like you've been making yourself available." She pushed back from the table and laid her bowl, mush and all, in the kitchen sink. "Now, I have work to do in the house today. You can stay around and help, or you can get ready and go to some classes. It's time. I'll give you until the end of the week if you need it, but we're both pulling ourselves out of this hole we've been in." Her voice rose just as mine had at the start of the conversation, ending on a note I could only call shouting.

It was the first time my mother had raised her voice at me since I was nine and flushed all her aquarium fish down the toilet to set them free. Later she'd apologize and say she was reacting to the stress and grief of Dad's death.

I knew it was Rhys' fault.

I didn't help her or go back to school that day. I lay on my bed, ruminating. Why did Rhys bother me? Why were Mom and I both drawn to him the minute we saw him? Me especially. I'd never reacted to a girl or guy that way before. He was hot by anyone's standard. Prince meets dark-eyed John Travolta. But this was more. His presence leaked into the brain. Hypnotic.

The question stayed with me when I turned up for classes the next day, hovered in the back of my brain as Mom and I avoided one another in increasingly smaller circles until we met for dinner at the kitchen table a week after Rhys' first appearance. She was humming as she took sausages off the stove and served them up with garlic mashed potatoes and carrots. Neither of us apologized;

we slipped back into a familiar pattern of evening catch-up about house renos and my computer studies, the only difference being how we both carefully avoided looking at the chair Dad used to sit in. I guess I'd been wearing my shoulders up around my ears for a few days because they were sore and sagging by the time we finished eating. It felt good to be us again, or as much us as we could be now.

Mom wiped her mouth with her napkin, tossed it on her empty plate and puffed out an almighty sigh. "I invited Rhys for supper tomorrow night."

My shoulder earmuffs returned. Dread whirled in my belly. Or was it anticipation? The absurd confusion of feelings kept me tongue-tied while Mom explained how he'd called to check in and wasn't that nice and he had a lawyer friend who'd be willing to talk to her about a wrongful death suit. "We're in a tight spot, darling. I can't sell the house until I'm finished renovating. Your father's salary used to pay for supplies to fix things up. We have some money saved, but it won't be enough. If Rhys' friend can help us…" The rest washed over me like a slow-rising tide. I understood the financial problem. That wasn't it. It was Rhys and how he was insinuating himself into our life. What was in this for him? Not like him and Dad were friends; I'd never heard Rhys' name before he turned up on our doorstep. He was a mystery.

"It's all right." I cut my mother off as she was running through dinner options that didn't contain onions or chives or leeks because Rhys was allergic. "I don't mind." I wanted to solve the puzzle. Right now, Rhys was one of those kids' deals with the big wooden pieces. The longer he stayed around, the quicker he'd turn into a 5000-piece jigsaw monstrosity. "Let's have him for dinner."

I tried not to think too hard about the time I spent styling my hair and picking out my clothes for dinner the next night. If pressed, I would've said it was a compulsion; a desire to be noticed. But it was way below the more urgent need to solve the Rhys riddle. He arrived early and I listened at my bedroom door to him and Mom talking for about twenty minutes before I joined them. He gave nothing away during their small talk, though my mother was having a high time (literally; she liked to enjoy a joint before supper), giggling at the stories he told her about Waterton. I came into the living room while he was in the middle of one about a colony of bats living under the Bannerman Avenue Bridge downtown.

"Hundreds of thousands of bats live there, since they renovated the bridge a few years ago. At sunset they fly out in this incredible cloud. Absolutely majestic." His dark eyes were more intense than I remembered, probably from the obvious passion he had for his subject. His hands were gesturing elegantly, like he was conducting the story as he told it. My mother was leaning toward him with her elbows on her knees, chin in her hands. She'd put on make-up for this event, I noticed.

"Bats are pests, aren't they?" I asked as I took a seat in the rocking chair. "Don't they carry rabies?"

"Hello, Finley." I could feel Rhys' gaze on me, but I kept my eyes on the smooth wood of the chair arms as I rubbed it. Getting pulled in by whatever charms he had wasn't going to help my mission. Impossible not to hear the dark, sinuous tenor of his voice, though. "You're not the only one who thinks that. Bats have an unfortunate reputation. People have been slow to come around to having a colony in the middle of the city, but the farmers outside city limits have started to sway public opinion. The bats eat pounds of insects every night, including crop pests. Nature's helpers."

"Fascinating," my mother said. It took every bit of muscle control I had to not to mimic her.

Rhys alluded to taking me and my mother to the bridge some evening to see the bats leaving the colony. The oven buzzer summoned us to dinner. The hair prickled on the back of my neck when Rhys pulled out my father's chair and sat in his place. I caught my mother's eye over his shoulder as my mouth opened to blast him, but she gave me the "please settle down" signal with her oven-mitt-clad hands. I snapped my mouth shut and nipped the edge of my tongue. A copper-tinged taste filled my mouth. Great. Rhys' head turned slowly in my direction.

"Are you all right, Finlay?" he asked.

"Yeah. Why?"

"You made a sound like you hurt yourself."

Did I? "No, it's nothing. I'm fine."

I swear he watched my lips move as if he had to read them to understand me.

"Hope you like pot roast," my mother said, laying a casserole dish with a hunk of beef and roasted vegetables on the table between me and Rhys. His attention shifted and I let out a huge breath I didn't know I'd been holding.

"It looks great, Madeline," Rhys said, so casually I wondered if I'd misread his intensity a second before.

"You weren't kidding when you said you made a mean…" He trailed off and his nostrils flared. "Is there garlic in there?"

"Yes! It's my pot roast secret. A full bulb goes in with the vegetables." My mother continued to pepper him with the tricks of her culinary arts, oblivious to the impossibly paler shade of white he was turning. "I used a little extra since I couldn't use onions or anything like that, because you're…Rhys? What's wrong?" She finally noticed what I had: the skin of his throat turning mottled scarlet.

"Allergic," he squeezed out before he stood jerkily and made his way up the hallway to the front door. He threw it open and continued to his Corvette where he leaned in the open passenger side window and, best I could tell, rummaged in his glove box. My mother was close on his heels, heaping apologies on him, hands flapping with her oven mitts still on.

I watched all this from the kitchen, my chair tipped on its back legs so I could see straight up the hall and out the open front door. The big wooden block puzzle pieces were shifting around my mind while I watched Rhys put something to his mouth and tip his head back like he was drawing in a deep breath. The pieces. The pieces. Garlic allergy. Pale, almost translucent skin. Worked night shifts at the hospital. Magnetic. My brain replayed the image of him staring at my lips when I bit my tongue. The skin all over my body puckered into tiny bumps.

I snapped my chair to the floor and pushed away from the table. Practically tore a trail in the carpet on my way to my bedroom. Dropped to my knees in front of my book-case. I scanned the titles until I found *Anatomy of the Vam-*

pire and flipped to the section I wanted. My finger traced the words as I sped through the lines: *A less well understood characteristic of the vampire is mesmerism: the ability to ensnare victims through mental manipulation…akin to hypnosis…categorized previously as a form of animal magnetism.* I sat on the floor with the book open across my folded legs. The puzzle pieces slid into place, locked.

Hello Rhys. Vampire.

My mother's reaction to my discovery ranged from, "I don't want to hear it", to "If you want to keep living here, you have to get help."

If only I could, Mom; Van Helsings don't grow on trees.

I knew she wouldn't believe me. She hadn't read what I'd read, didn't live in the folkloric worlds of words I'd immersed myself in for years. I told her because I wanted to be able to say later I tried to warn her — not in an I-told-you-so kind of way, but so she'd understand why I had to protect her.

The plan required careful preparation. First, I had to diffuse Mom. She wanted me to get help. I did. On paper. I told her I set up an appointment with a psychiatrist, left the house for the appointment, went for a walk in the park across town, and came home refreshed. She also wanted me to make room in my life for Rhys, because he was being such a good friend to her. I did. On the surface. I nodded in the right way when she said he was coming over, encouraged her to use the shampoo I'd laced with holy water on the evenings she would see him, made mundane small talk with him. Knowing what he was banished the hypnotic pull he'd had on me in the beginning. My heart still kicked up a notch when I heard his voice and my eyes continued to follow the smooth grace of his movements, but it was different; I imagined myself as a tiger watching a grazing deer through the tall grass. Tail twitching. Waiting for its moment.

Mom wanted me to concentrate on my studies. I did. Not the ones she meant. I deferred my college courses for the semester, but carried on like I was going to school every day. I hit the big library on the university campus instead. The literature on vampires – folklore to fiction – had so many contradictions. I needed to get as close as I could to an agreed-on set of facts about their habits and strengths. Their vulnerabilities. Robinson (1889) claimed vampires always turned a victim after one bite, but Joyce (1901) said vampires could choose to feed off victims without ever turning them. Agarici (1818) - vampires can fly; Montgomery (1905) - vampires can't fly. Brown and Brown (1921) held the unconventional belief a vampire could transfer its consciousness into a victim at the time of biting and infection, jumping from one body to another. Newton (1843) disagreed; vampires remained trapped in the same body, at the same physical age they were when infected. I was relieved when I read in Charteuse (1919) that vampires don't have adverse reactions to crucifixes and silver; until then, I couldn't reconcile Rhys' vampirism with the sight of the small silver chain and cross he wore around his neck.

The research was silent on how long it took a vampire to decide the fate of a victim – turn them or feed on them

– but I sensed a restlessness in Rhys that made me feel he was getting tired of playing with my mother. He started coming over less often and, when he was at the house, checked his watch constantly. I know because I never took my eyes off him from the minute he arrived until the door closed behind him.

While it conflicted on many points, the literature did agree on one fact: a wooden stake through the heart was the only sure way to kill a vampire. The local hardware store had a sale on wooden garden stakes. Five for a dollar. I picked up ten. I counted out quarters at the cash, thinking where I could place the weapons around the house: one in each bedroom, of course, and at the front and back doors; the pantry in the kitchen; under the couch in the living room.

"Did you say something?" the cashier asked. She was a stout woman in her fifties, frowning at me behind big round glasses attached to an eyeglass chain around her neck. I shook my head and looked around me, behind me. I was alone in the lineup. She kept glancing up at me as she pushed the quarters into her palm with the edge of her other hand. When I got back in the car, I looked at myself in the rearview mirror. Sure, the bags under my eyes were set deeper than usual, more purple, and I probably should've combed my fingers through my hair before I went in, but seriously, lady, not like you were cashing out someone from *One Flew Over the Cuckoo's Nest*.

What's that saying? God laughs while humans make plans? No idea or scheme or strategy I was putting together came close to how it ultimately went down.

The details are etched in my brain. It was a Friday night. Mom had agreed to rent *Poltergeist* and watch it with me. She was really taking one for the team considering the last video we watched, *Blade Runner*, wasn't even scary and her fingernails were chewed down to nubs by the end of it. As we were settling in, the phone rang. I could tell it was Rhys by the soft pitch of my mother's voice and the way she twirled the curly cord of the receiver around her finger while she spoke. She asked me if we'd like to go see the Bannerman Avenue Bridge bats with Rhys (could the man be any more obvious?). I bit my lip and considered. Any mention of Rhys shredded my nerves, and here he was wedging himself into my movie night, but Mom seldom left the house and I hadn't yet had a chance to hide the wooden stakes in each room. I was quiet for so long, Mom started to tell Rhys no, we already had plans, but I interrupted and told her to go on without me. "We can watch the movie later," I said. "I'm tired. Maybe I'll take a nap." I forced a yawn.

As soon as she pulled out of the driveway, I was off the couch and throwing aside rolls of landscape fabric and garden pots in the back of our shed to pull out the stakes. I followed the plan I'd laid out, placing one in any room where it could be well hidden. I worked my way into the living room, where I lifted the skirt on the bottom of the couch and slid the last stake into place. Good thing I worked fast, because the headlights from my mother's car shone into the living room window seconds after I was done. I threw myself into the rocking chair.

"That didn't take long," I said as she came in the door.

She looked around and frowned. I scanned the room, hoping I hadn't left anything out of place.

"Did you cook something while I was gone?" she asked, putting her keys down on the table by the door, instead of on the wall hook where she usually hung them. "Smells like onions or something."

As if I'd had time to cook anything. I stuck my nose in my armpit and grimaced. Maybe that's what she was smelling. "Nope," I said. "How come you're back so early?"

She flopped on the couch and explained how Rhys had to leave, he'd started feeling ill. "Just as well. The bats weren't very active. A man next to us said he'd heard from a friend on city council that someone might've poisoned the bats on purpose. Who would do that? People are sick."

Poor Rhys. A family emergency!

"That's not funny, Finlay," Mom said. I didn't realize I'd spoken out loud.

"Sorry." Head down. Had to stay in character.

She leaned across the arm of the couch and touched my hand where it was sitting on the arm of the rocking chair. Her fingers were frosty. I had to slow my rocking so her hand didn't fly off mine. "Are you okay? You're soaking wet."

"I'm fine. I was thinking about a school project while you were gone. Big one. Semester's almost over." I ran my free hand through my hair, pulling through the tangles.

"The accident...it hasn't been that long. You shouldn't push yourself so hard." She released my hand to cup my cheek. "You look exhausted. Are you sleeping?"

I shrugged. Her cold hand was comforting on my warm cheek. I leaned into it. She was talking about grief and rest and asking when I had a shower last and it all flowed together into one softly rippling string of words. Until she said my name.

"Finlay? Are you listening? What about Dr. Metzer? Money is tight, but the lawyer Rhys set me up with thinks we have a strong case against the hospital. They might settle a case with us quickly to keep things out of the news. You could have some extra appointments if you need them."

I stopped rocking. Opened my eyes. Her deep brown ones were staring into mine.

"Finlay? Hellooooo?" Her cupped palm came around my chin and waggled it gently. I snapped my hand around her wrist and squeezed. "Ouch! Stop! What—"

"Darling," I said. I stood up and forced her back so she was sitting squarely on the couch. Her eyes flicked back and forth between mine. "My mother never calls me Finlay. She always calls me 'Darling'."

"Fin—" she cleared her throat. "Darling. Stop. This...I don't know what this is, but we can fix it. We can get help."

"Cold as death, don't know where to put your car keys. 'Smells like onions or something.' You practically hypnotized me in the chair a minute ago. What was the plan, get me in the jugular while my eyes were closed?"

My mother opened and closed her mouth like a gold-fish. She shifted and the light reflected off the necklace she was wearing, one I hadn't noticed until now. I laughed, high and biting. I couldn't help it; it was so absurd.

"You even kept that?" I asked, pointing to the thin silver chain and tiny cross. "Come on, man. You played such a good game all this time and you gave it away in overtime!"

"Rhys. Gave it to me. I've been wearing it for a week, Finl...Darling. Sit down. Please. Let me go. You're hurting me!" It screamed when I twisted its wrist. "Please..."

"This was the last thing I expected you to do, Rhys." I started to kneel on the floor and turned its wrist hard enough to feel the ligaments rolling over the bones. My mother's legs – its legs, Rhys' legs, I corrected myself - kicked out at me and screamed words my mother would never use. I bent far enough to reach under the couch skirt, felt around until my fingers grazed wood. "When you got tired of playing with her, with us, I figured you planned to infect her. Change her. But you seemed to have a thing for her, so then I thought you might just feed off her for a while and let her go." My hand closed around the stake. "But you went with transference! Moved yourself right into her body. You don't read about that much in the lit- erature. Maybe not all vampires can do it? Stop it. You're going to break her wrist. Ha! Like it'll matter in a minute. No bite mark on her neck, hey? Smart. Better to hide it somewhere more discreet."

I yanked on its arm and it rolled off the couch and landed on its back next to me. I was up, my hand jumping from its wrist to its throat, sitting on its stomach before it could recover. It gurgled; hands clawed at my wrist. I understood an occasional word: don't; stop; love. The rest was a wet, choked mess of sounds.

"I thought you'd be stronger. Most of my research says

vampires have super-human strength." I raised my other hand and it saw the stake for the first time. The mother-Rhys creature bucked like a rodeo bull trying to throw a rider. "I guess it takes time for whatever it is that courses through your veins to spread through her body." I looked at the blood under its nails where they'd torn my skin, the red skin swelling around my fingers on its throat, its bulging brown eyes.

"You took her," I said to it. "The only thing I had left."

I brought the stake down, hard and fast.

The irony of me being here is not lost on me. When I was a kid, I used to imagine myself settling down in one place, but it was always somewhere exciting, like London or Sydney. Los Angeles. Waterton wouldn't have made it onto the longest of long lists, let alone this old building that occupies one tiny corner of the city. I've been here for a couple of months and it's not a bad place. My room is comfortable and gets sun in the morning. I get to do group activities. The food sucks, but the meds I'm on don't leave me much of an appetite. The orderlies are nice, except the one that pretends to be Rhys. He used to come up to me when I was alone in the yard. He'd squeeze my arm too hard or sneer names like "flippity-Fin" and "mother-killer" into my ear. I told my doctor about it. He nodded and scribbled on his notepad; told me he'd make sure it never happened again. The next day my blue pill was gone and I had a new pink pill. The Rhys imposter hasn't come near me since, but I think I've seen him at the end of a long hallway, or across the yard, watching me.

Even though things have been going well, I can't sit still for long and am finding it hard to concentrate on the books I'm allowed to read. Summer is coming. The doctor said it will be too hot on the top floor of the hospital and me and the other patients are going to be moved to the basement for a few weeks. The same basement where my dad died. But that's not what's bothering me. It's my mother. Or, the thing that used to be my mother. It hovers outside my window most nights. How did I miss its heart with that wooden stake? I checked for a pulse after, but it's not like a vampire has a heartbeat.

I recognize the fluttering ivory dress it has on - my mother wore it to my high school graduation. The glass is too thick for me to hear anything, but I can read its lips. "Darling," it says.

7

"What did I just watch?" Scott said.

"Good sir, we took a trip to loony land," Jad replied.

"There are days I could strangle my mother, but Jesus," Sasha said.

"I don't want to look at the stone," Kinna said.

"Hell with that," Jad said. "I need to know whose name is on it." He stepped to the front of the gravestone. "Ha. I wasn't expecting that."

"Don't say it!" Kinna said, holding her hand up. "Seriously, I don't want to know, Jad. Don't ruin it for me. I want to decide for myself what happened to them all."

"Bravo, Ms. Chaytor," Cinn said, clapping his hands.

"You can have that mystery all to yourself, Kinna," Sasha said. She leaned over the back of the stone and read the inscription upside down. "Well. Scott, check this out."

Scott glanced at Kinna. "Sorry, Kin." He let go of her hand to check out the epitaph. "Oh, wow. Wow. You sure you don't want to know?"

"I'm sure," Kinna said. "It doesn't matter whose name is written on it anyway. How would we know for sure they were actually buried there?"

"What do you mean?" Sasha asked.

"I mean, vampires wouldn't stay buried, would they?"

Scott tilted his head and said, "Kinna Chaytor, do you believe vampires are real?"

"You do not," Sasha said.

Kinna put her hands on her hips. "So what if I do? You think horoscopes are real." She pointed at Scott, "You think Area 51 is an alien compound."

"The evidence—"

Kinna cut Scott off and nodded at Jad. "And you. Any luck catching the boogeyman on the night-vision camera you set up in the old rectory your uncle bought?"

Jad put his hands up. "Hey girl, I'm with you."

"Sorry. Anyway, I don't want to know. Please don't tell me."

Scott, Sasha and Jad looked at one another, then at Kinna. In that moment of stillness, all four became aware Percivet Cinn was still clapping. A slow regular rhythm.

"You can stop now," Kinna said.

The clapping continued. Cinn's image flickered, enlarged to twice its size, and shrank back to normal, hands still moving together. The sound became distorted, echoing like the clap of a hundred pairs of hands instead of only one.

"Hey, Percy," Jad called over the clamour.

Scott cupped his hands over his ears.

"That won't stop it," Sasha said. "It's in your head, remember?"

"Cinn! Percivet Cinn!" Jad kept yelling.

"Ahh!" Sasha sagged against a nearby tombstone. "We have to shut down the apps on the phones!"

"Mine's dead," Scott yelled over the escalating noise. The tenor was becoming like the clang of a bell.

"Mine, too," Kinna said. Sasha and Jad pulled theirs out and shrugged. Dead.

"Is anyone else's token heating up?" Jad asked, fingers rubbing the back of his neck.

"Take them off!" Kinna shouted. Her teeth were humming. A throb started at the base of her skull, radiating from the Virtoken. She picked at the disc, getting her fingernails under its edge. She pulled and it stuck like a tick anchored to her flesh. A firm yank and she yelped in pain. The disc came away. She held it up in front of her face. Her fingertips were dipped in blood. Cinn was gone and the sound had stopped.

For her.

Scott was curled on the grass, hands clasping his head, moaning. Kinna saw the disc still attached to his neck, the skin around it red and swollen. She scrambled over Sasha and Jad, who were a tangle of arms, trying to help each other get their tokens off, and she forced Scott onto his stomach, digging her fingernails into his neck as she'd done to herself. When the disc ripped free, it left an angry, raw spot on his neck. Scott's body went limp under her, in relief or unconsciousness. Kinna whipped around to find Sasha and Jad. They were leaning against a tall white tombstone with a cross on top, bloody Virtokens in the crisp white gravel at their feet. The devices looked like two tiny, black, bloated leeches in the circle of their flashlight beams. Kinna rolled off Scott, chest heaving, and lay on the ground with an arm over her eyes. Cool moisture from the grass seeped through the back of her jacket and shirt. She didn't care.

"Are you two all right?"

Kinna's ears were ringing so fiercely she couldn't tell who said it. A suggestion of light crept in around the bend in Kinna's elbow and she moved her arm. A flashlight hit her full in the face and she cursed.

"Sorry." Sasha. "Is he alive?" Kinna could hear fear even though Sasha was trying to keep her tone even.

"I'm here." Scott's muffled voice seeped out around the blades of grass sticking in his mouth. "Is he gone?"

Kinna, Sasha and Jad did a full circle scan. No sign of Percivet Cinn.

"Yeah, gone," Kinna said. She rested her head back on the ground. Scott, Sasha and Jad talked above her, Sasha's excited exclamations contrasting with the boys' deeper tones. Directly over her a small pocket had opened in the fog and she could pick out the shimmering light of dozens of stars. The sight of openness took the edge off her agitation. Her breathing slowed. As it did, her mind wandered back through the evening: the sensory hangovers from the sims, Cinn's increasingly aggressive attitude, glitches in his program. Her gut had been trying to tell her something was wrong, that the tech was off. She talked herself out of it each time. That pissed her off. Only at the end, when the tokens had a meltdown and they couldn't disengage the hardware from the app, did she do anything.

Kinna sat straight up. "Oh my God."

"What? Where?" Jad swung around, squatting in a fighter's stance. Sasha's flashlight jerked crazily. Scott slowly lifted himself onto one elbow.

"The phones. I didn't even realize."

"What? Where?" Jad repeated, staring into every pocket of darkness around them.

"Our phones were dead," Kinna said. She got to her feet.

"Yeah, we know," Scott said. He probed the back of his neck and sucked in a breath when his fingers touched the oozy patch where the disc used to be. "I've got a hole here because you had to pull the token off instead of just switching the apps off. And, by the way, it's a major design flaw that you have to skin yourself to remove one."

"They went haywire," Sasha said. "Did you feel how hot they got?"

"Guys, stop. It's not even that. The tokens were connected to our phones. The phones ran the apps. The apps were connected to the server. You need all of it to run Cinn and the story simulations."

"And?" Sasha said.

"Oh my God," Scott said, echoing Kinna. "My phone was dead before we even got to the last story. And your battery was low ages ago; it probably died in the middle of the sim."

"I don't know when mine died," Sasha said. Jad shook his head.

"So how could we see Cinn and interact with him and go into the simulation without a connection to the Cramon Cemetery app? How were we doing all this for the last half hour with dead phones?" Kinna's stomach clenched as she looked from Sasha to Jad to Scott. Their expressions ranged from confusion to horror.

"That is an excellent question, Ms. Chaytor."Kinna closed her eyes and hoped she was the only one who heard his voice. At least that would mean he wasn't real, even if it did mean she was having a mental breakdown.

"You can't be here." Kinna tensed all over when Sasha spoke. Her hands and feet started to tingle when Jad added, "I'm not the only one who can see him, right?" Every cell in her body screamed at her to run when Scott rolled to his feet and said, "We have to get out of here."

"Now, children. Do not rush off. You have almost completed the Cramon Cemetery Experience."

Kinna cracked an eye like she did as a kid to check if the scary part of a movie was over. The first thing she noticed was she could see deeper into the cemetery. The fog had thinned. Not a wisp swirled around the tombstones or the figure weaving his way through them. Percivet Cinn came to them in full colour this time, his jacket a deep emerald green, the waistcoat under it eggplant purple. The pants were charcoal, almost as dark as his black boots. Skin the colour of ashes, hair black as the sky above them. He could pass for a real person - one with a dated sense of fashion – if not for the fact he left no boot prints in the damp grass.

He stopped in front of Kinna. "You said you wanted to finish the experience, did you not?"

Up close, she saw the only remnant of the blue-light version of him: his eyes. Deep, flickering indigo.

"Changed our minds, Percivet. Thanks for the offer, though." Kinna noticed Jad used Cinn's full name, not the shorthand that had annoyed their host throughout the night. Thank you, Jad, for not poking the bear.

"I have a confession to make," Cinn said. He folded his hands at his waist and hung his head a fraction.

"Let me guess," Scott said. "You wouldn't have let us quit."

"Exactly. Forgive my insincerity. It is always easier if—"

Sasha's fist swiped through Cinn's face from behind, obscuring his pencil moustache and moving lips. He turned his eyes on Sasha. "Rude," he said. Her head jerked. She groaned and fell to her knees, clutching her nose. "It is quite unpleasant when someone does it to you, would you agree Ms. Balakov?"

Jad swore a streak at Cinn any sailor would be proud of and kneeled next to Sasha. He moved her hands away and a trickle of blood ran from her nostril to her top lip. Kinna saw the run of emotions on his face as if they were printed on his forehead: concern, anger, fear, rage. The last one had him balling up his fists and coiling his body to strike out.

"Jad, don't," she said. "You'll make it worse." She didn't understand the mechanism, but Cinn obviously had the ability to manipulate things in the physical world if he could cause Sasha to experience what amounted to a punch to the nose.

"Please listen to her, Mr. Erim. Your only option is to see the experience to its conclusion."

"But we did finish it," Scott said. He was at Sasha's side, helping her to her feet while Jad supported her on the other. Kinna took a step toward him and the four friends stood shoulder-to-shoulder facing Cinn.

"The last star on the map was the vampire story," Kinna added.

"That was your last simulation as an observer, yes. But you still have one more experience ahead of you. I promise it will be far more immersive."

"We're done, we don't want any of this." Sasha snorted and spit a glob of bloody saliva through the toe of Cinn's boot.

Kinna jumped in before Cinn could react. "How is any of this possible? We took out the Virtokens. They weren't even working the way they were supposed to. How are you here?" Kinna could hear the rising pitch and speed of her own voice. *How, how, how?* Why was this happening? Were they having a group hallucination? That could happen, right? Oh shit, were they dead? Did they die in a car accident on the way here and were trapped in limbo? She tried to stomp on the panic sprinting along her nerve endings. Scott grabbed her hand and squeezed, anchoring her. She concentrated on the steady pulse coming through his hand to hers.

"Does it matter?" Cinn said. "I could tell you the tokens allowed me into your heads, but would that satisfy you? If I tried to clarify the neurological nature of it, could you comprehend it?" He raised his pointed eyebrows high above his eyes, inviting a response. "Exactly. I believe we have gone beyond the need for explanations. What matters now is what we do next." He paced in front of them like a drill sergeant sizing up recruits. "The question I have been asking myself as I observed you this evening is, which experience would best suit you four? You have a high tolerance for the physically grotesque and the psychologically perverse. What challenge can I give you that will truly have you earning your prize?"

"What prize is that?" Kinna asked, knowing already this evening's events pointed to one answer.

"Your lives, of course," Cinn said.

"What is this, *The Hunger Games?* Everybody needs to calm down." Jad's hands were ruffling his hair into spikes.

"I am quite calm, Mr. Erim. Your friends appear calm. It is you who needs to take several deep breaths."

Kinna wouldn't say she was calm, but she'd had the advantage of expecting Cinn's answer. Scott's lack of reaction made her wonder if he'd suspected it as well. As for Sasha, hard to know if she was too angry to absorb it or too busy talking Jad down to process it.

"And how does it work?" Scott asked. "If we die in the simulation, we die in real life? How would you manage that?"

"So many ways, Mr. Mahoney. For example, if I tweak the immune system just so, it floods the body with chemicals that do the most amazing things to the body." Cinn held Scott's eyes and cocked his head. At the end of their little line-up, Jad's rambling denials of their situation stopped. A dry, rasping sound replaced it. His fingers grabbed at his throat and Sasha tried to keep his big frame upright as his knees buckled. Hives broke out across his cheeks and the backs of his hands. She screamed Jad's name, pleaded with Cinn to stop.

Scott ran to Jad's side, hands fluttering over him, unsure what to do. "I get it!" Scott yelled, swinging around to Cinn. "Please, let him breathe."

Cinn straightened his head.

Jad coughed and sucked in an enormous breath. He rose to his hands and knees. Sasha leaned close, slipping soothing words into his ear. Kinna watched Cinn watching the trio. Her heart sank when his expression shifted to a deep curling smirk that lifted the ends of his moustache.

"I have decided," he said.

Blackness started at the edges of Kinna's vision, closing in from all sides. She saw her three friends kneeling together on the ground in the last speck of light. Then, nothing.

THE TIES THAT BIND

They arrived in the middle of band practice. Trumpets and trombones bleated. A deep bass drum set a heavy beat for a set of tittering Tom-Toms and clashing cymbals. Crowds cheered. Car horns beeped?

Maybe not band practice.

Kinna opened her eyes. She was standing at the edge of a sea of women, men and children. All ages. A white-haired couple stood with their backs to her, the man waving a tiny paper flag. The backs of heads as far as she could see up and down the sidewalk. Except for a couple of curious kids, probably five or six years old, perched on their fathers' shoulders, who twisted around to look at her and the three people on the ground in front of her. Jad was on his hands and knees, Sasha squat down next to him, her arm across his back. Scott was bent over them both, his hands hovering.

"*Semper fi*, baby! Whoot, whoot!"

Kinna turned. A man in his early twenties with his shirt off and a U.S. Marines tattoo on his pectoral was standing on a bench behind them. He pumped his arms in the air, hooted and called out the Marines' slogan again.

She jumped onto the bench next to him. At this height she could see past the crowd, into the street. A band in red military jackets with wound white rope capping the shoulders marched down the street, playing the upbeat, martial tune. Behind them, a float decorated in giant paper pastel flowers rolled along the street. A half-dozen men in stark white shirts sat in a low rowboat nestled in the flowers, paddling as if they were on water. A dark-haired woman in a fuchsia sari trimmed with gold stood among them, waving to the crowd.

Floats, dance troupes, and bands stretched up and down the street as far as Kinna could see. A parade. Lots of people, big vehicles. Too many moving parts for Kinna to hazard a guess at why Percivet Cinn dropped them here and what scenario they were being forced to play out.

"Damn, girl, those legs tired? Because they've been on my mind since last week." The shirtless idiot standing next to her finished his nonsensical pick-up with a hearty beer-reeking belch in Kinna's face. She put a hand in the middle of his chest and pushed him over the bench's backrest. His head met the concrete with a hollow *pop*. He didn't get up.

"Christ, Kinna, what'd you do that for?" Scott was standing in front of her, eyes level with the band of skin exposed by her cropped top and low-rise jean shorts. He'd tried to look up at her when he spoke, but his eyes kept drifting to her pierced belly button.

"Godsakes, Mahoney, focus! Here, help me down." She snapped her fingers to nudge him into reaching up for her hand. He did, but kept his eyes straight ahead. "He's not real," she said in answer to his question. Her feet hit the sidewalk. "There's nothing there to hurt. And he was a dickhead." She gave Scott a once-over. "What are you wearing?"

He had on a banana-yellow tank top with the word "SLUT" printed under an image of a pineapple in a pink thong. Blue cargo shorts peaked out from under the shirt's long hem. Brown flip-flops finished the look.

"I have no idea. I came to like this. You're one to talk, Teen Vogue. How can you even walk in those?" He pointed to her four-inch stiletto heels.

"I can't," she said. She bent down and measured her foot against the unconscious guy's sneakers. Not a bad fit. She untied them and slipped them onto her bare feet. She shoved one of the stilettos into Scott's hands and kept the other one for herself.

"Why are you giving me this?" Scott said, holding the shoe by the very end of its pointed heel like it was going to attack him.

"They'll have to do until we can get our hands on better weapons."

"I've got my eye on a metal cane someone left leaning against the bus shelter," Jad said as he and Sasha joined them at the bench.

"Jad, you can't do that," Sasha said.

"He can. And you have to, too." Kinna waved her hand to take in everyone and everything around them. "All of this is a simulation. None of these people are real, none of them matter. There are probably consequences for our actions – I'm sure we can get arrested if we get caught doing something illegal – but nothing we do here matters back in our own world. Except surviving."

"Right, I know," Sasha said. "Sorry. It's so realistic, I have to keep reminding myself it's only in my head. I can feel the wind on my skin!"

"So much skin," Jad said, pointing at Sasha's miniskirt, off-shoulder t-shirt, and strappy sandals.

"You're one to talk," she retorted. Jad looked down over his naked torso, down his mid-thigh brown shorts, and brown leather sport sandals.

"Why the hell are we all dressed like this?" Scott asked, pinching his pineapple's thong between two fingers and holding the shirt out for the others to inspect.

"To blend in?" Sasha suggested. "We're like anyone else here our age; they're all dressed for the heat."

"Heat and tight shorts don't mix," Kinna said, grabbing the back of her shorts to pull them out of her butt. Did that perv Cinn put her in boy-cut underwear? God, she hated those. On the second grab, she felt something crinkle in her back pocket. A piece of paper. She read out what was written on it: "It says, 'Sunset. Eight hours.' Succinct when he wants to be. At least we have a timeframe."

"We should go somewhere quiet, get oriented," Jad said. "I don't like being in the middle of this crowd. He could throw a million different things at us out here."

A faint scream reached Kinna's ears. "Seriously, Jad?" she said. "It's like you invited him to kick it off."

"I think the scream came from that direction," Scott pointed in the direction the parade was heading. "Go the other way?"

They all moved where he pointed without replying. Jad snatched the metal cane on their way by. Kinna heard a second piercing scream over the pop-music thrumming out of the nearest float. A murmur passed through the crowd. Several people stood on their tippy-toes, angling their heads to look down the street. She split her attention between the sidewalk in front of her and scanning the storefronts they passed by, looking for one they could go into. Preferably one selling things they could use as weapons.

"Argh! Why is everything closed in the middle of the day?" Jad said. "It must be a holiday here." More screams echoed off the buildings. The people on the curb started talking louder. "Here Sash, you take this." He handed the cane to her. "No! Please don't argue. I'll pick up something else."

Kinna spotted a young boy at the edge of the crowd tossing a rock in the air and swinging at it with a junior-sized baseball bat. She snatched it out of his hands as the four of them sped by and tossed it to Jad. A subtle wave of movement passed through the parade watchers, as if a giant gust of wind hit them. Several had to take steps back to keep their balance. A couple of families detached from the group and started to walk in the same direction the four of them were heading. More filed in as the next wave of movement came. The sidewalk got so full, it got hard for spectators in the crowd to step onto it, so they turned around in the mash of bodies along the curb and tried to weave their way through. The bands in the parade stopped playing. Floats turned off their music. Louder, shriller screams came more frequently until they were a constant score for the increasing crush on the sidewalk.

"We have to find somewhere, fast," Jad said. He was

breathing hard. Sweat beaded at the band of his back-wards-facing baseball hat and dripped down his face.

Kinna remembered in that moment how Jad wouldn't go to stadium concerts or get into a crowded elevator. The swarming of the crowd had to be torture for him. She felt a shove against her spine and looked back to see a thick herd of humanity pressing up the sidewalk behind them. She was forced to trot to keep from having her heels stepped on. She grabbed the hem of Scott's shirt. "Hold on to each other!" She had to yell at the top of her voice to be heard over the unending cacophony of screaming and shouting.

"We should try to get into one of the alleys," Scott called.

Someone started running. It set off a chain reaction in the crowd. The pace accelerated. Kinna worried about Sasha, the shortest out of the four of them, being able to keep up if the speed picked up. The thought raced through Kinna's mind at the same moment her own foot caught on an edge in the sidewalk. She stumbled, arms flailing. Scott's shirt slipped out of her grip. She heard him call her name and told them to keep going when he tried to turn back. The sound of two gunshots resonated off the brick buildings lining the street and the crowd surged. Kinna stayed on her feet but was propelled forward and side-ways by the swarm of people until she came up against a hip-high flower box built around a light pole. Perfect, Kinna thought, climbing onto the lip of the box and hold-ing the pole for balance. She scanned the throng and saw Scott's beacon of a shirt disappear under a bright blue aw-ning attached to a tan brick building. He never came out the other side. Good. They were waiting for her, or finally found an open shop.

A new sound crept in under the screaming surrounding her and Kinna swung around to look down the street. The tide of people moving toward her filled the street from storefront to storefront. About a block away, the tide wavered, clumped, clustered. People were bunching; fighting, Kinna thought. The new sound rose in volume. It reminded her of the rolling vibration a dog makes deep in its chest before attacking. The clusters advanced and spread through the herd. They left things behind on the pavement as they moved. Hard for Kinna to make out. She knew each second she stayed on the box made it harder to find her friends, but finding out anything she could about this scenario Cinn had them in would help them survive it.

So she watched.

In less than a minute, a scuffle broke out among a knot of people at the end of the block, no more than three bus-lengths away. The guttural growling was loud enough that Kinna could hear its slavering, wet quality. Screaming assaulted her eardrums. Arms swung and fists flew violently between the fighters. She saw several blood-soaked hands. More blood than she'd expect in a fist-fight. Were they using knives? The cluster broke open and Kinna saw the blood- and gore-ringed mouths of the people left standing. Saw the red heaps of bones and viscera they left on the pavement behind them. A shock ran through her spine, ending at the base of her skull, where all the fine hairs stood on end.

"Fuck."

She spun and launched herself into the river of sweaty bodies speeding by her, breaking into a run as soon as her feet hit the sidewalk. She pushed people from behind, shoving them to their knees, even the ones carrying small children. The growling became a roar, almost drowning out the screaming. *No, there are just fewer left to scream*, Kinna realized. Her eyes stayed focused ahead of her, looking for a bright blue awning on a tan brick building. When she reached it, her heart sank. The store it belonged to was boarded up and covered in graffiti. Scott, Jad and Sasha were gone. The thought came and went in the two seconds it took to run past the building. Maybe they doubled back and she missed them? Maybe they got caught by... nope, her mind wasn't ready to say the word yet. She had to believe her friends were ahead of her.

An explosion shook the ground. People around her gasped and turned to look. Kinna kept going. The more people she could put between her and what was coming up the street, the better. Her lungs were burning and the muscles in her legs were trembling. She wasn't sure how much longer she could run.

A flash of yellow up ahead. Scott's shirt with its ridiculous pineapple, waving in the air like a flag, over the heads of the freaking, stampeding mob. She caught sight of him on Jad's shoulders and in spite of everything, smiled at the sight of the two of them, knowing they waited for her. Scott saw her, dropped his flag and waved his arms like a crazy man. He started to smile back, but it froze on his face. His eyes widened and he started slapping Jad on the head and scrambling to get down. She didn't see what happened next; a yank on her shirt from behind pulled her off her feet and she landed flat on her back on the concrete. The breath whooshed out of her lungs and into the face leaning over her.

Lips drawn back in a snarl, face smeared crimson from its chin to the bridge of its nose, flecks of flesh and muscle stuck on cheeks and forehead, eyes black and lifeless.

Even with her mind howling the truth, she couldn't accept what she was seeing. Even when she swung her shoe up in an arc and the spike of her stiletto entered the thing's temple and it gurgled and dropped limp on top of her, she couldn't believe it. Not even when the thing's dead weight was lifted off her and she scooped the blood out of her eyes to see Scott standing over her, holding out his hand, could the reality sink in.

Only after he'd pulled her to her feet, they'd pushed their way to the door Jad held open, and she'd sat on the floor, her arms wrapped around her knees, could she admit that son of a bitch Percivet Cinn had sent them into a zombie apocalypse.

"Was that a—"

"Yes."

Scott dropped down next to her. "Oh no. No, no, no, no."

"Yes."

"What's going on out there, Kin?" Sasha asked.

Kinna filled them in on the slaughter in the streets. The animal sound of it. The empty creature that dragged her down on the sidewalk.

On the last word, she let go of her knees and lay back on the floor to stop the spinning in her head.

"Zombies?" Sasha threw her hands up. "How the hell

do we survive that?"

"Don't get bitten and aim for the brain," Scott said.

"Any guesses at how many hours we have left?" Jad asked.

Scott shook his head. "We'll track the sun."

"Whether we've got six hours or two, seems to me we're in triage," Sasha said. "We don't need a lot of supplies. I'm tired and thirsty, so looks like this sim forces us to take care of bodily functions: eat, drink, rest."

"Weapons, food, water," Kinna mumbled. She rubbed her temples with her fingertips. Scott put his hand on her shoulder and kneaded the muscles.

"Medical supplies; bandages, antiseptic," Jad added.

"Maybe a map," Scott threw in.

Kinna raised her head. "Can we get any of that here?"

"Maybe some," Sasha said. "It's an office building. The directory says it's mostly law firms. We're in the lobby. That set of stairs there goes up to the other floors. Probably another set of stairs over there that go to the basement." She pointed to a door at the back of the lobby with a stair symbol and a downward arrow. "We don't know where that door on the side goes. Probably into the building next door."

A squelching smear on the front window made them jump and swing their heads toward the sound. A shadow shuffled by the frosted glass, dragging something along the window that left a long, streaked wavy line of red.

"It's gone quiet," Kinna said.

Besides the squeal on the glass, there were no sounds. The screaming had stopped.

"I hadn't noticed," Scott said.

A part appeared to fall off the shape outside the window and the squealing stopped, too. The shadow kept moving.

"What if we barricaded ourselves in here," Scott said. "From what Kinna described, we're facing hoards out there, no matter when we leave. If we can protect ourselves here, it's as good a place as any to wait it out."

"Cinn won't let that happen," Kinna said.

"You're right," Jad said. "He wants us on the move." He rolled his head, stretching the muscles in his neck. "I think we need to look at this as a race: we're trying to get to a finish line; that's the only safe place. Anything that doesn't get us closer to that is a waste of time."

"And more dangerous," Kinna added.

"So, we stay on the move," Sasha said. "I still think the first thing we do is loot this building." She waited for their nods before taking Kinna by the hand to help her up from the floor. "We'll take the top two floors, you guys get the rest."

"Thank God for health nuts," Kinna said, zipping up a running jacket over her crop top. The jogging pants were too short, but luxuriously comfortable compared to the short-shorts she'd arrived in.

Sasha double-knotted the laces on the sneakers she'd found in one of the bathrooms and rolled up the cuffs on a pair of jeans. "We lucked out compared to the guys."

Jad was knotting the ends of a cut-off black barrister's robe around his waist. The sleeves billowed out at his elbows, where he'd had to trim them. "I look like a samurai who went through a paper shredder."

"Dude, at least you don't look like a kid wearing his dad's clothes." Scott rolled up the sleeves on a blue suit jacket that hung off his shoulders. "Another human could fit inside here with me. But at least I got rid of the flip-flops. Those are death traps. Lucky for me a hulking woman worked here." He extended his foot and examined the pink running shoe.

"Could've been a guy who was really passionate about breast cancer awareness," Sasha said.

Kinna picked up a backpack off the floor and slung it over her shoulder. Another knapsack and two courier-style bags remained. "I divided up the food and drinks as evenly as I could, except for the two extra water bottles I put in Jad's bag. You're the biggest, so I gave you the extra weight."

"My curse," he said, adjusting the strap of the bag across his chest.

"I think I can get rid of your stiletto now that we have the golf clubs," Scott said. He swung the heavy iron experimentally. "With the clubs, the bat, and the couple of steak knives we found, we should be good, but if anyone sees an outfitters store, shout it out."

Sasha shook her head as she settled her bag on her shoulder. "Look at us, at what we're doing." They glanced at one another, taking in the motley mix of clothes and the make-shift weapons gripped in their hands. "If I try to absorb what's happening, it's like a giant vice starts to squeeze my head. This is insane. All we did was go to a stupid VR simulation."

"And now we're trying to avoid being zombie food," Kinna said. "I know. I start to think about it and it winds me up so much I can't breathe."

"Me too," Scott said. "I'm trying to stay in the moment."

"I imagine crushing Percivet Cinn's head with this bat," Jad said. "Keeps me focused." He swung it in a wide, sweeping arc.

"Guys," Kinna said. "I have to tell you, if we don't make it, there's nobody I'd rather—"

A series of thumps battered the door off the side of the lobby, punctuated by a trio of withering screams. The four of them turned with their weapons raised. One more muffled thump and the door cracked around the knob and swung open. A short middle-aged man stumbled into the lobby and hit the floor on his hands and knees. He looked up at the four teenagers staring at him.

"Please," he moaned before a grey-haired couple staggered through the door, clothes and flesh coated with gore, and fell on him, biting into the exposed skin on his neck and arms. His screams were ear-splitting.

Jad took a step toward them; Sasha stopped him with a hand on his wrist. "Not real, remember?"

"Come on. Stairs." Kinna ran to the door at the back of the lobby. She hit it on the move and the four of them pounded down the narrow stairs. They ended at a hallway only wide enough for them to walk single-file. A door with a glowing red exit sign was at its end. It was open, moving back and forth on creaky hinges. There were two open doorways along the hall, neither lit. Kinna turned and put her finger to her lips and signalled to the others to size up the hallway. They all nodded. She took a breath, raised her golf club in one hand and steak knife in the other.

One step at a time, on the balls of her feet, she moved forward. She sensed the others on her heels. The only sound in the hallway was the creaking of the door and the light scuff of their shoes on the dirty tile floor. At the edge of the first doorway, Kinna poked her head around the jamb and back for a split-second look. It seemed to be a bathroom. She took a slower peek and confirmed it was empty. She moved on. The next doorway was closer to the exit. They crept forward. Two steps from the door, a hollow plinking stopped them in their tracks. It had come from that room. Kinna tried to deepen her breath to control it. In through her nose, out through her mouth. She clenched her jaw. The sound came again as she got to the edge of the doorway. She raised the knife; changed her grip on the blade so it was sticking out of the bottom of her fist and she could jab it forward into an eye or throat with more force. A quick check around the doorjamb, like before. A small supply room. Clear, she thought. She did a slower check. A spray paint can rolled on the floor from the small breeze coming in the door. *Plink-plink.* Her shoulders sagged and she huffed a choppy breath out of her mouth.

The exit door sent out a long, groaning creak. She heard Scott yell her name at the same moment a slavering growl bore into her brain. The creature at the exit door caught the sleeve of her jacket in its clawed hand and pulled her through the opening into the alley outside.

If Kinna hadn't had the knife up, if she hadn't been ready, the zombie's mouth would have descended on her face before she had a chance to jam the serrated blade into its eye socket. She relived the moment and other possible (less fortunate) outcomes in a loop as the four of them sat silently in blood-soaked clothes inside a taxi stand, leaning against the dispatcher's desk as they shared a bag of potato chips.

Their escape up the alley had been trial by fire. At least a dozen undead had been milling around the dumpsters and stacks of pallets dotting the narrow garbage-strewn space. Kinna's tussle with the first one had the rest of them closing in on her, Jad, Scott and Sasha in a loose circle. The baseball bat and golf clubs cleaved into blood-streaked faces, open chest cavities and gaping brain cases with surprising precision for a bunch of novice zombie killers. If she hadn't seen it for herself, she never would've believed Sasha could swing a 9-iron hard enough to cave in the temple of a grown man, even an undead one. There'd been a dicey moment near the end, where Scott went down and a prone creature they thought was dead snagged him by the collar, dragging him toward its chattering teeth. Jad stomped on the thing's head and exploded its skull a second before it chomped into Scott.

"I don't know if I can do that again," Kinna said.

"I'm exhausted," Jad added. He shook out his robe-shirt and chip crumbs scattered across the floor, along with a tooth.

"We have to keep moving," Sasha said. "This place is too small. A group of them could probably tip it over. And there's no room in here to swing at anything."

Scott reached up on the desktop behind him and pulled down a map.

"Saw this when we came in," he said. He spread it on the floor between his splayed legs. He pointed to a red circle. "I'm guessing that's the stand we're in." He dragged his finger down the street west of them. "They've marked major stops on all the roads. See down this way, there's a hardware store. Further down, a bank." He looked up at the small window at the back of the stand. "The sun is definitely getting lower. If we get to the hardware store, we can upgrade our weapons. Then we hit the bank. That's probably the safest place we can easily get to and take a proper rest. We can pick our next stop from there."

Kinna giggled.

"What? You don't agree?" Scott asked. His tone was defensive.

"I do. Really, I agree. I just had this sudden image of you commanding an army. You're a natural; look at how you sized this place up in a hot minute. Remember a million years ago when we were wandering around a graveyard thinking about going home because Jad had a boo-boo on his knee? Now we're strategizing about how to defend ourselves against zombie hoards. Remember? Remember how it was all my idea to do something scary in a cemetery? Ha,ha." Kinna felt the hysteria bubbling up but couldn't do anything to stop it. It surged through her, forcing out more high-pitched giggles. Jad asked if she was all right, Scott reached for her knee. The laughter kept fizzing. Overflowing. It crashed and she exploded into shoulder-heaving sobs, covering her face with her hands.

"Nobody blames you," Scott said. He folded the map and slid it into a pocket on his backpack. "I put on my big-boy pants and decided all by myself to do the sims."

"I'd have been pissed if we never went ahead with it," Jad added.

"I'm so sorry," Kinna sniffed.

"It's not your fault, Kin," Sasha said softly. "We all had a feeling something was wrong with the tech, any of us could've left, but we all decided to stay."

Kinna continued to sob, but more gently. Within a few minutes, sniffles took their place. She took her hands away and wiped her nose on a discarded credit card slip she found on the floor. "God. Sorry about the pity party." She hiccupped. "It's just…everything."

"Are you kidding?" Scott said. "You were the last one. Sasha had her breakdown while we were hoofing it up the sidewalk hours ago. Me and Jad had mini-meltdowns while we were looting the lawyers' offices."

"Not cool, man. We agreed not to tell anyone."

"Yeah, yeah," Sasha said. "Big tough guy. Like I didn't notice your eyes were red when you got back." She leaned into Kinna's shoulder. "Whatever this is, however it happened, the people responsible are outside this sim. We'll find them when we get out. They're going to get their asses sued off."

"Or worse," Jad said, flexing his sticky red hands.

Kinna rubbed her cheeks with the sleeve of her jacket, drying her face, leaned her head back against the dispatcher's desk and closed her eyes. "Thank you for being awesome." She felt three hands come together over hers and heard at least one of her friends sniffle. She smiled.

"Good to go?" Scott asked.

Kinna nodded and they got to their feet together.

"Crap." Jad was looking out the plate glass window over Kinna's shoulder. "Gotta go, right now."

Kinna settled her bookbag on her back and checked the window. A group of bloodied bodies in cheerleader uniforms was staggering its way from the other side of the street. "The parade just keeps on giving," she muttered. Packed up and armed, they left the stand through its only door in full view of the oncoming zombies. The low hum from their mangled faces rose to gurgling growls.

"This way," Sasha said. She darted into an alley behind the taxi stand. Jad followed, then Kinna and Scott. They kept their pace to a slow trot, listening for scuffing, clanging; anything suggesting movement. At the end of the alley, they craned their necks around the side of the building to check up and down the street. A low melody was playing nearby. A few undead were bumping into each other way up one end of the street, opposite the direction they needed to go. On the route they were headed, two parade floats were angled across the road, blocking parts of the sidewalks.

Sasha went first. They stuck to the middle of the street to keep away from grasping hands or hungry mouths reaching out from doorways or alleys. The closer they got to the first float, the louder the music got. The volume was turned low, but the words were audible.

Four green and speckled frogs
Sat on a speckled log

The float was built on a trailer with a thick fluttering fringe of tinsel around its base. Paper Mache palm trees decorated the top, supporting a banner reading, "St. Gerard's Elementary School". When they got closer, Kinna saw mounds of bones and guts dotting the fake grass covering the trailer bed.

Eating some most delicious bugs
Yum, yum!

They weren't real people, she reminded herself. Part of the sim.

The trailer was attached to a tractor with tires almost as tall as Jad. The low connecting point between the two was the only place to get past the obstacle without climbing over the gory float or the enormous farm vehicle.

One jumped into the pool

Sasha stepped over the steel hitch, light as a bird. Kinna was next. They had to keep moving to make room for the boys in the narrow space between the vehicles. Sasha looked both ways.

Where it was nice and cool

When she lifted her foot to step out, a hand shot out between the rasping tinsel strands concealing the space under the trailer. Kinna's mind registered the next seconds in snapshots: the exposed bones and muscles in the hand contracted when they grabbed Sasha's floppy pant leg; a second, smaller hand curled around her ankle; they pulled together; Sasha fell forward to the ground, snapping her chin off the pavement; a third hand, broad and hairy-knuckled caught Sasha's other leg; Kinna, Scott and Jad tangled with each other, trying to grasp a hand, a piece of clothing, anything to hold her, all of them shouting in tandem; Sasha catching Kinna's eyes, hers wide and disoriented, as her entire body was hauled under the trailer with one massive pull.

Then there were three green speckled frogs.

Jad dropped next to the trailer and yelled Sasha's name wildly. Each one of her moaning screams drove up his volume until he was hoarse. The whole time, Kinna and Scott struggled to hold his legs, put their weight on him, to keep him from crawling under the trailer.

"Jad! You can't! Stop!"

"Let me go! I can get her!"

"She's gone. Listen."

The only sound was wet mastication.

"She's dead. Jesus. She's dead." Jad said it over and over again, still fighting them.

Scott got him by the arm and twisted it behind his back. Grunting with the effort to hold it without hurting Jad, he said, "If anything comes out of there now, it won't be her."

"Jad, we can't stay." Once Scott had Jad by the arm, Kinna got up and started gathering the bat and golf clubs they'd dropped. She scanned the street in both directions.

Ahead of them a handful of zombies had come around the side of the second float. Behind, undead were filing out of the alleys. "More are coming. You have to get up. Right now."

"She's dead, she's dead." Jad continued the refrain. Kinna grabbed the skin on the back of his thigh and twisted it as hard as she could. Jad roared like a beast and rolled, flipping Scott onto his back with an *oof*. He came up on his feet, facing Kinna like a linebacker. His expression was pure, blind fury.

"You going to die too, there on the ground? The things under there are starting to move and there's a pack of them coming down the street. We. Have. To. Go."

Jad grabbed his hair and pulled until his eyes watered. Scott scrambled out of the way as he stomped in a tight circle, screaming throat-grating rage into the unaffected and disinterested air. He snatched the bat out of Kinna's hand, wound up, and smashed it against the tractor's window. Kinna and Scott stepped back to avoid flying shards of shattered glass as Jad brought the bat down again and again until the bat broke and all he held was the jagged-ended handle. His whole torso rose and fell under the strain of his breathing.

The sounds under the trailer got louder.

"Jad! JAD! Come on." Scott took a chance on grabbing Jad's arm again. No resistance. He towed him, lumbering, up the street toward the second float, both of them following Kinna's lead.

"We've got five to get through," she called to them. She tossed Scott a club and raised hers. Scott left Jad on his own and swung at the skinless face of the limping woman closest to him. Kinna took down two more. The fourth was a giant. They worked together to get him to his knees, then Kinna took her knife out and drove it into his brain through his ear.

"That's four. Where's five?" She whipped around. A zombie was back-on to her, right in front of Jad, hiding him from her view. Its head was moving rhythmically, like it was chewing. "No!" She lunged, but stopped short when a jagged object broke through the top of the zombie's skull. The corpse fell to the ground. Its head was skewered on the broken bat handle from the bottom of its jaw to the top of its head.

Jad looked at her. "Throw me a golf club."

It landed in his palm with a slap and he took off running.

"He's going the right way, so I guess we follow him?" Scott asked. They took off in Jad's wake.

The screaming at the float – Kinna couldn't think of it as the place Sasha died, not yet – had stirred up a convoy of the undead. She'd thought their way would be clear after they passed the second float, but the mob thickened. Jad sawed a path through everything that got between him and a step forward.

"I'll jump in if it gets too hairy, but I'm afraid he's going to clock me with that thing if I get close."

Scott said what Kinna was thinking. Jad didn't seem to be too discriminating about where his 7-iron was landing. They gave him room and he used his golf club to bathe himself in the spattered brains and bone chips of any zombie that wandered their way.

Kinna checked behind them for any nearby undead.

She never looked too hard at their clothes or faces. If she saw Sasha she was afraid her mind would crack once and for all. She noticed the sun was low, casting long shadows of streetlights, cars, and anything else on the street in front of them.

"I think we should skip the hardware store and go straight to the bank," Kinna said, breath coming fast and hard from the continual running.

"We're getting low on weapons," Scott said. He was winded, too. They parted to jog around either side of yet another car dead in the middle of the street.

"I know," Kinna said. The bat was long gone. Scott had abandoned his club minutes before when he couldn't wrench it out of the chest cavity of a lone flesh-eater who'd come at them out of the cab of a truck. "But look where the sun is. We probably only have a couple of hours left. I think we can lock down the bank for most of that time. If we have to leave before the sun sets, at least we'll be rested."

"Could be weapons at the bank," Scott panted. "Guns. Let's do it. Do we need to tell him?"

"No need. Jad will keep mowing in a straight line until we tell him to stop. You know the map. Let me know when we're getting close."

He scanned the storefronts as they jogged by. On the corner up ahead, an orange plastic awning angled out over the sidewalk. "That's the hardware store," he said. "The bank is on the next block, on the far corner."

Ahead, Jad had slowed to a trot. There was one lurching shape ahead of him, striking in its red uniform jacket and stark white shoulder decorations, but the road beyond was clear from what Kinna could see. She tapered her jog down to a walk and Scott fell in beside her. They were both huffing hard. Kinna's scalp prickled with sweat trying to make its way to her hairline.

"Jad, hold up!" Scott called. Jad put the finishing touches on the zombie-brain marmalade he was making with his club in the skull of the former marching-band member.

He looked up. Kinna shivered.

"Can you imagine that coming at you out of the dark?" she asked Scott. Jad was a blood-stained creature out of a nightmare. He'd torn off his lawyer's robe ages ago when it got too wet and sticky. The insides of too many zombies to count were spattered in his lank hair, down his bare chest, and across his shorts and bare legs. His sandals squished moistly as he approached them.

"I can. And shortly after I imagine me shitting myself lifeless. That's who you want by your side in this fight, though." Scott raised his hand at Jad when he got near. Kinna thought he looked like he was greeting a neighbour over a backyard fence. It was so ludicrous, but so fundamentally Scott, affection for him welled up inside her.

"What?" Jad said when he stopped in front of her.

She realized she was smiling and got serious. Fast. "Nothing. Thinking about getting out of here."

He didn't respond. There was no sign of jovial Jad; that guy stayed behind at the float with Sasha. Not that Kinna blamed him. It was hard enough for her to think of Sasha; for him, the loss must feel like a hole carved through his core.

"Yeah, so the bank," Scott said. "It's up ahead."

"No hardware store?"

Kinna explained to him the rationale she and Scott had for going straight to the bank. Jad sized up the position of the sun and nodded. He tightened his grip on his golf club and headed toward the end of the block.

The intersection was clear of people, undead or otherwise, but the pavement was visibly cluttered with debris. As they got closer, Kinna saw what she'd taken for garbage was actually musical instruments. Horns, drums. A marching bell - one of those giant xylophones played in marching bands – standing straight up in the street, wobbling. What a perfect symbol for this shitshow, Kinna thought: a giant set of metal ribs. As they neared, Kinna saw its pole was jammed partway into a manhole cover. The wind picked up and the wobbling got more erratic.

"We need to run," she said, hair standing on the back of her neck. The boys didn't need urging; they'd noticed the tilting noise-maker, too. The moment they took off, the bell teetered too far to recover and clattered onto the pavement. The clang of metal meeting asphalt echoed across the block. Kinna pictured the sound spreading out in a circle, like rippling shockwaves, waking up every empty-eyed almost-corpse in town.

They skidded to a stop at the corner, in front of the bank doors. Scott went straight to them and pulled. Kinna looked up and down the street they'd entered. The size of the surging, writhing crowd of zombies approaching from both directions was staggering. She realized they must've circled back to the original parade route. Ground zero.

"They're locked!" Scott screamed. He had a door handle in each hand and was throwing every ounce of his weight into pushing and pulling them. They didn't move an inch. Kinna scurried over to grab a discarded saxophone off the street and swung it at the glass door. It bounced off with enough force to tear itself out of her hands.

"Jad, get up here and help. Jad?" She looked around. No sign of him. Goddamn idiot! Did he think he could go and fight them all off by himself?

The sound that had become the soundtrack to her fear, the snarling of the undead, got louder. She didn't look, didn't want to know how close they were getting. Her eyes met Scott's instead. His jaw was clenched, veins pulsing at his temples from strain. Here they were. At the end. And her only realizing that night, hours ago, how important he was to her. After so many years of friendship. She swallowed hard. The revolting gurgling of the hoard was almost on top of them, blocking out all other sound.

Except the horn.

Blaring in an unending, ear-splitting honk, it rose in volume by the second. A pick-up truck bore down on them. Kinna saw Jad in the driver's seat before her and Scott lunged to the side and the truck collided with the bank doors, crushing them inward in a spray of glass. She and Scott rolled to their feet and climbed through the wreckage. Kinna hissed as she tore the flesh on her hands and arms trying to push through the twisted mess. She scanned the inside of the bank in a beat, saw nothing moving. Her eyes settled on the perfect place for them to go. She turned back to the truck. Behind it, frayed, bloodied bodies – grasping, growling - were piling against what was left of the bank's windows and the crimped metal door frames. There were so many of them, they jammed up open spaces large enough to fit through, slowing them down, but one would slip through any second, opening the floodgates for the rest.

She bolted for the driver's door of the truck.

Jad was pushing feebly, trying to get out. His forehead was gushing blood from a four-inch gash. Scott was already yanking at the door. Metal ground against metal as he heaved it open. He popped Jad's seatbelt and the heavy bloody mess of him fell out of the truck cab.

Scott slung Jad's left arm over his shoulder. Kinna slipped in under the other. She ground her teeth together and her face thrummed with pressure from the strain to lift him. He was dead weight.

"Come on, Jad," Scott yelled over the cacophony of grinding metal and animal growls. "Need some of your steam to move you, buddy." Glass shattered behind them. "Oh shit!"

Three lurchers staggered in before the mob jammed up the opening again. Scott tried to turn to face them, but slipped on the shards of glass spread across the floor. He grunted and shouted a string of curses. The move worked in his favour: instead of taking the three of them head-on, the slip caused two to stumble over him. One did them the favour of face-planting onto a piece of jagged door frame and laid still. The other went to his knees next to the truck. While Scott spun to face the third zombie, still cursing a blue streak, Kinna slid out from under Jad's arm and grabbed the open truck door from behind. The kneeling zombie lifted itself to reach for Jad's outstretched arm. Its head came into line with the truck door opening and Kinna threw all her weight into slamming the door shut, crushing the thing's head against the unforgiving metal frame. She opened it and slammed it closed twice more for good measure, screaming like a banshee. The creature dropped to the floor, it's head pulpy. She turned in time to see Scott, bloodied and battered, kneeling on the zombie's chest, smashing its head into the tile floor until a gooey mass flowed out the back.

They both converged on Jad again. He was rolling his head, moaning. Kinna leaned off and slapped him across the face as hard as she could. His eyelids shot open like they were on a switch. "GET UP!" she screamed into his face.

Out of the corner of her eye, she registered Scott's punch-drunk expression. He leveraged himself under Jad's arm again. She did the same. With Jad's help, they were able to get him on his feet. "The vault," she said, grinding the word out through the strain it took to keep Jad going. She steered them toward the tellers' wickets and the small room behind them filled with safety deposit boxes. Its thick metal security door was open. So was the gate of heavy steel bars that was usually closed and locked during a bank's business hours. Kinna envisioned an enterprising bank employee rolling the dial on the combination lock and swinging the gate open in the hope of snagging cash or valuables in the confusion of the zombie breakout.

The pounding and crunching at the bank doors melded into a single rolling rumble before giving way to screaming metal and breaking glass. It sounded like the whole front of the bank collapsed inward. *How close? How close?* Was the hoard surging around the pick-up truck?

Flooding the lobby of the bank? Her brain screamed at her to hurry.

Relief almost made her legs give out when they crossed the threshold of the vault. She gave into it as soon as they laid Jad on the floor in a semi-conscious heap; slumped next to him. Scott stayed on his feet.

"Close it," Kinna managed, shutting her eyes to stop the spinning in her head. The heavy gate clunked as it met its frame. The combination lock whirred as it spun, locking them in. In spite of the rising sound of the hoard, her lips curled in a weak smile. "Think we did it," she said. It was all she could manage.

"You did," Scott said. So far away.

"Come here," she said.

"I can't, Kin."

She cracked her eyes open. Looked up when she didn't see him nearby.

"What did you do?" she said, adrenaline giving her one more hit to lift her to her feet, propel her to the gate, where Scott was standing on the outside. Dozens of shapes shuffled in the shadows behind him.

"They got me." He held out his forearm for her to see the wide bite mark, so red it was almost black.

"But it's almost over! You could still make it. It could take hours to change you. You don't know!"

"Or it could take minutes. I couldn't trap myself in there with you and take that chance." His breathing picked up. He looked over his shoulder at the snarling silhouettes closing on him. Back at her. She grabbed the bars of the gate. She let the heat burn behind her eyes but held back the tears that would soothe it.

His hands were shaking when he laid them over hers. "You know, right?" He searched her eyes.

"I do," she said. "And you? Do you know?"

He smiled and nodded. Swallowed hard.

A phantom face appeared over his shoulder, ghostly white. A gaping red hole sat in the middle of its face where its nose used to be. The lips were gone, chewed off by itself or another creature. It hissed and snarled. Scott pushed away from the gate and spun around with his elbow up. The thing fell back when he connected with its head. He reached for the edge of the vault's solid metal door and pulled. It swung until it sat on the door jamb, unlatched, but cutting off the sights and sounds outside.

Kinna wasn't sure how long she stood in the silent black void before her hands slipped from the gate and she slid to the floor.

EPITAPH

The light was blinding, even behind her closed eyelids. She turned her head to try and get away from it. When that didn't work, she tried to lift her arm over her eyes, but something tugged on the back of her hand and she couldn't get her arm all the way over.

"Best to keep your arm down, honey. You don't want to pull out your IV." A gentle hand guided her arm back to a soft surface. "Janice, can you tell the doctor she's awake? And call the parents. They're probably already on their way back from getting coffee, but best let them know so they don't delay."

A warm cloth settled over her eyes.

"Try this. You open your eyes with this on and the light won't sting so bad."

Kinna did as she was told.

Better.

She fluttered her eyelids, waking them up. She lifted the corner of the cloth and let in more light. Pale walls came into focus. And a whiteboard. "Your nurse's name is Cynthia" was scrawled across it in black marker. She let the cloth drop back on her face.

"Cynthia."

"That's right. How are you feeling, Kinna?"

"How did I get here?" Kinna asked, ignoring what was a complicated, maybe unanswerable, question.

"An ambulance brought you and your friends in."

"Friends? They're here?" Warmth blossomed in her chest. Cynthia was quiet for several seconds. "Maybe it's better to talk when your folks get here."

Kinna lifted the cloth off her face and turned her head toward the slender chestnut-haired woman sitting next to her.

"Cynthia. If you don't tell me where my friends are, I'm going to roll out of this bed and go down every hallway, crawling if I have to, until I find someone who will."

"That's…well. That's something." The nurse cleared her throat. "Big man is down in the ICU. He's in a coma."

Jad made it. Kinna squeezed her eyes shut and thanked someone, something, for making it happen. But she need-ed to know it all.

"Sasha? Scott?" Her voice caught on his name.Cynthia sighed and Kinna heard her shift in her seat. "I'm sorry, honey. They were gone before they got to the hospital."

Dead.

Thinking the word made bits of her reality crack and float away; little hot air balloons of her sanity abandoning her.

So she decided not to think it. Sasha and Scott away, that's all. Somewhere else.

She rolled in the bed, gave Cynthia her back. The movement activated every nerve in her body, sending spasms of pain through her limbs, her back. She groaned. Her head felt like a sun-ripe grape ready to split its skin.

"Careful, Kinna. Your body had taken a beating. Go slow."

Instead, she'd think of Sasha and Scott as somewhere else. Away. That's all.

After a minute, she heard Cynthia stand up. Her soft shoes made gentle squeaking sounds on the floor as she headed for the hallway. "Press the buzzer if you need anything. I'll be out at the station." Kinna could tell she was closing the door by the gradual muting of the sounds coming from the hall. Before it shut - over the nurses' chit-chat, the pings and dings of the ward – Kinna thought she heard Cynthia singing.

Two green and speckled frogs…

ACKNOWLEDGEMENTS

Matthew LeDrew, Ellen Curtis and everyone at Engen Books: thank you for believing I had it in me to finish a book and seeing the potential in this one.

Ali House: thank you for your merciful, but thorough, editing touches.

Thank you to members of The Naked Parade Writing Collective with whom I've had the honour to work: Angela Antle, Sarah Bennett, Bridget Canning, Diane Carley, Terry Doyle, Penny Grimm-Hansen, Matthew Hollett, Jen McVeigh, Heidi Wicks. Your talent, insights and workshopping wisdom have pushed me to be a better writer.

Thank you to the Writers' Alliance of Newfoundland and Labrador for creating an open, accepting space where aspiring writers can feel like they aren't alone.

My family and friends cannot be acknowledged frequently or loudly enough for their support not only throughout the writing of this book, but also during the years of change and challenge that preceded it. In particular:

Andrea Furlong, Jennifer Janes, Alicia Beresford: thank you for reading drafts, coming to launches, always asking what I'm working on and how it's coming along, being patient when I go into hiding for weeks at a time on a writing binge, and being overall awesome human beings.

Amanda Labonté: you deserve all the gin for all the ways you've helped me keep my sanity throughout the past five years of writing adventures.

Thank you to my brother, whose feedback on the stories in this book and encouragement during their writing kept me going when I was convinced it was all crrrrrap.

To my parents, who put books in my hands from the moment I was old enough to hold them and read them to me until I could read them myself: your unwavering belief that I should be a writer is the gift that got me here today.

Finally, Jeff. Thank you for saying, "Yes, I absolutely agree it's a great idea if you quit your job, change careers, and start writing books." I can't imagine being on this journey without you.

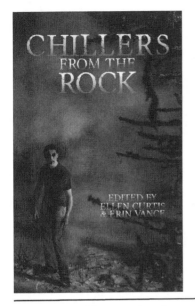 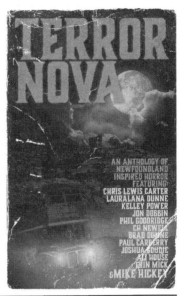

Did you enjoy the work of Kelley Power?
Read her other short fiction in Engen's bestselling anthologies,
including *Terror Nova* and *Chillers from the Rock*.

Also featuring the work of Ali House (*The Segment Delta
Archives*), Matthew LeDrew (*Coral Beach Casefiles, The
Xander Drew series*), Jon Dobbin (*The Starving, The Risen*),
Brad Dunne (*After Dark Vapours, The Gut*), international
bestseller Paul Carberry (*Zombies on the Rock, Carcharodon*)
and many more!

These collections showcase the talent, imagination, and
prestige that Canada has to offer. From stories of censorship
gone awry to sentient buses, global warming to corporate-
branded culture, these collections have it all!

Kelley Power is an award-winning author whose work has appeared in *Chillers from the Rock* and *Terror Nova* (which was an Amazon Canada #1 Best Seller in Horror Anthologies). Kelley writes from her home in St. John's, Newfoundland and Labrador.

www.kelleypower.ca

Made in the USA
Columbia, SC
07 October 2022

69007004R00138